The kiss meant nothing.

Nothing at all.

That's what Serena had been telling herself ever since last night when she'd fallen into Jackson's more than capable arms. What had she been thinking to kiss the enemy?

Who was she kidding? Jackson wasn't the enemy, even if he was part of the news media. Maybe at first she hadn't trusted him—with her background, who could blame her? But during the time they'd spent together, she'd learned that there was so much more to him than his dashing looks and his news coverage.

He was a man who'd loved and lost. He was kind and generous. He went out of his way for others, even when he'd rather be doing anything else. And he had a sense of humor. The memory of his deep laugh still sent goose bumps down her arms. That was a sound she could listen to for the rest of her life—

Whoa! Slow down.

She knew that this moment of playing house would end soon—just as soon as the avalanche was cleared and they were able to plow the roads. Then they would return to reality. But for now they had their own little world within the walls of this cabin, and she intended to enjoy it as long as it lasted.

And if that should include some more kisses?

Well, she wouldn't complain. A smile pulled at her lips.

She'd been kissed by a lot of leading men, but none of them could come close to Jackson. That man was made for kissing. Just the memory of his kiss had her sighing. It hadn't lasted long enough, not even close.

Dear Reader,

Sadly, there is no GPS for life. Sometimes you get lucky and pick the right path and other times you'd give anything to go back in time and pick the other. And sometimes the hardest path is the one with the most rewards.

Grab a cup of cocoa and join sexy and famous Jackson Bennett in *Snowbound with an Heiress*. He has taken a wrong turn in the Alps. Christmas is fast approaching and he's lost in a snowstorm. He's certain that his stroke of bad luck couldn't get any worse. But you know what happens when you think that...it does! Get worse, that is.

But movie-star-in-hiding Serena Mae Winston is there to save the day. And then to her horror, she realizes she's just saved one of television's biggest news anchors. She's certain it's the worst thing to happen to her.

Forced together in front of a crackling fire with a sweet puppy named Gizmo, Jackson and Serena must ride out the storm. Perhaps the Christmas season is the perfect time for them to learn to trust again, and so much more...

Happy reading,

Jennifer

Snowbound with an Heiress

—

Jennifer Faye

ISBN-13: 978-0-373-74457-2

Snowbound with an Heiress

First North American Publication 2014

Copyright © 2014 by Jennifer Faye

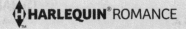

HARLEQUIN® ROMANCE

Printed in U.S.A.

Recycling programs
for this product may
not exist in your area.

ISBN-13: 978-0-373-74457-2

Snowbound with an Heiress

First North American Publication 2017

Printed in U.S.A.

Award-winning author **Jennifer Faye** pens fun, heartwarming, contemporary romances with rugged cowboys, sexy billionaires and enchanting royalty. Internationally published, with books translated into nine languages, she is a two-time winner of the *RT Book Reviews* Reviewers' Choice Award. She has also won the CataRomance Reviewers' Choice Award, been named a Top Pick! author and been nominated for numerous other awards.

Books by Jennifer Faye

Harlequin Romance

Mirraccino Marriages

The Millionaire's Royal Rescue
Married for His Secret Heir

Brides for the Greek Tycoons

The Greek's Ready-Made Wife
The Greek's Nine-Month Surprise

The Vineyards of Calanetti

Return of the Italian Tycoon

The Prince's Christmas Vow
Her Festive Baby Bombshell

Visit the Author Profile page
at Harlequin.com for more titles.

For Tonya.

Thanks for being there from the beginning...

I am thankful for our friendship and your unending encouragement. :)

Praise for
Jennifer Faye

"This one had my emotions all over the place. It's funny, tender, heartbreaking...definitely a book you want to read."

—*Goodreads* on *The Greek's Ready-Made Wife*

"Ms. Faye has given her readers an amazing tearjerker with this novel. Her characters are relatable and so well developed...it made everything come to life right off of the page."

—*Harlequin Junkie* on *The Prince's Christmas Vow*

CHAPTER ONE

PEACE AT LAST...

Serena Winston paused along the snowy path. Out here in the beauty of the Alps, it was so quiet. She lifted her face up to the warmth of the sun just seconds before it disappeared behind a dark cloud. Shadows quickly spread over the mountainous region of Austria.

She sighed. The sunshine had been so nice while it lasted, but the snow was starting to fall again. But she had to admit that the snowflakes had their own charm as they fluttered to the ground. It was so different from her home in sunny Hollywood.

"Arff! Arff!"

"Okay, Gizmo." Serena glanced down at her recently adopted puppy. "You're right. We better keep moving."

There was already plenty of snow on the ground. Serena's fondest wish had always been to learn to ski, but for one reason or anoth she'd kept putting it off. First, it was due to the worry of injuring herself before filming a movie. Being an actress did have its drawbacks. And then, there just wasn't time to jet off to Tahoe for a long weekend of skiing—especially now that she'd inherited her legendary father's vast estate. Selling off some of his holdings was more complicated than she had anticipated.

Realizing the direction of her thoughts, she halted them. She drew in a deep, calming breath. This holiday excursion was meant for escaping her daily pressures and refocusing her Hollywood career. There was yet another reason for this spur-of-the-moment trip, but she didn't want to think about it, either. There'd be time for problem-solving later.

When she glanced back down at her teddy bear dog, she found he'd wrapped his lead around a bush. The easiest way to fix the situation was to release Gizmo from his lead. It was no big deal. Gizmo was not one to wander off.

Serena unhooked the lead. "Stay," she said firmly.

Gizmo gazed at her as though understanding what she'd said. He didn't move a paw.

"Good boy."

Serena set to work untangling the leash from the prickly shrubbery. It wasn't an easy task.

What had Gizmo been doing? Chasing something?

At last, she freed the leash. She'd have to be more careful about letting him out on the full length of the lead in the areas with rougher terrain.

"Arff! Arff!"

She watched as her little dog took off in hot pursuit after a brown-haired creature. "Gizmo! Stop!"

Serena ran after the dog. She continued calling his name, but he paid her no heed. For a little guy with short legs, Gizmo could move swiftly when he was motivated enough. And right now, he was very motivated.

Serena wasn't familiar with the terrain, as this was her first visit to the small village nestled in the Austrian Alps. This area had been on her bucket list to visit right after Fiji and right before Tasmania. With her rush to leave Hollywood, it seemed like the right time to scratch another adventure off her list.

The snow grew heavier. Between the snowflakes and trees, she spotted a road ahead. And though it appeared to be a quiet road, the thought of little Gizmo being anywhere near had Serena pumping her legs harder and fa

"Gizmo—"

Serena's foot struck a tree root. Down she went. *Oomph!*

The collision of her chest with the hard, frozen ground knocked the air from her lungs. She didn't have a chance to regroup before she heard the sound of an approaching vehicle. With each heartbeat, the sound was growing closer.

Ignoring her discomfort, Serena scrambled to her feet. "Gizmo! Here, boy."

She continued after the little furbaby who'd captured her heart a few months ago. At first, she hadn't been so sure about owning a dog. Gizmo was full of puppy energy and in need of lots of love.

But now she couldn't imagine her life without him. Gizmo made her smile when she was sad and he made her laugh when she angry. Not to mention, he got her up and moving when she thought she was too tired to take another step. He was there for her unlike anyone else in her life.

It wasn't like Gizmo to take off and not listen to her. She supposed that between the long flight from the States and then the intermittent snow showers that they'd been cooped up inside for too long.

The blast of a horn shattered the silence.

It was followed by the sound of skidding tires.

A high-pitched squeal confirmed Serena's worst fears.

Her heart leaped into her throat as she came to a stop.

A loud thud reverberated through the air. And then the crunch of metal sent Serena's heart plummeting down to her new snow boots.

A whole host of frantic thoughts sprang to mind. They jumbled together. The immobilizing shock quickly passed and she put one foot in front of the other. All the while, she struggled to make sense of the tragedy that undoubtedly awaited her.

As if on autopilot, she cleared the overgrown path. She scanned the quiet road. Her gaze latched on to the back end of a dark sedan. Inwardly she cringed.

And to make things worse, there was no sign of Gizmo.

Or maybe that was a good thing. She was desperate to cling to any sense of hope. She held her breath and listened for a bark—a whimper—anything. There were no puppy sounds.

Please let Gizmo be safe.

Steam poured out from the engine compartment of the crashed vehicle. The driver's side was bent around a cluster of trees. Serena's mouth gaped. Was that the reason G didn't respond? A sob rose in her throat. Was he pinned in the wreckage?

Tears pricked the back of her eyes. *Please, say it isn't so.*

Moisture dampened her cheeks. She swiped at the tears. For a normally reserved person who only cried on a director's cue, Serena wasn't used to a spontaneous rush of emotions. Realizing she couldn't just stand there, she swallowed hard and then moved forward, wondering what she would find.

On legs that felt like gelatin, she moved across the road. Realizing the driver's-side door was pinned by a tree trunk, she approached the passenger side and yanked open the door.

A snapping and popping sound emanated from the car. Serena didn't even want to imagine what that might be. Still, she glanced around for any sign of fire.

Not finding any flames, Serena knelt down to get a better look. There in the driver's seat was a man with dark brown hair. His head was leaned back against the seat. His eyes were shut. His dark lashes and brows gave his face a distinctive look. There was something familiar about him, but in her frantic state, she couldn't make any connections. Right now, she had to get this man to safety in case his car went up in flames.

Even though she'd played a nurse once in a

movie, she didn't know much about first aid. The movie had been a stalker/thriller type. The medical aspects were minimal. She reached for the cell phone in her back pocket. She pulled it out, but there was no signal. This wasn't good—not good at all.

"There…there was a dog…"

The deep male voice startled Serena. His voice wobbled as though he was still dazed. She glanced up to find a pair of dark brown eyes staring back at her. Her heart lodged in her throat. Was it wrong that she found his eyes intriguing? And dare she say it, they were quite attractive. They were eyes that you couldn't help staring into and losing yourself.

The man's gaze darted around as though trying to figure out what had happened. And then he started to move. A groan of pain immediately followed.

"Stop," Serena called out. "Stay still."

The man's confused gaze met hers. "Why? Is there something the matter with me?"

She could feel the panic swelling between them. "I'm not sure." She drew in a calming breath. Getting worked up wouldn't help either of them. She drew on her lifetime of acting. "I don't know the extent of your injuries. Until know more, you shouldn't move." Which all well and good until the car caught f she could only deal with one catastrophe at a time. "I'm going to call for help."

"You already tried that. It didn't work." His voice was less frantic and more matter-of-fact.

She swallowed hard. So he'd seen that. *Okay. Don't freak out or he'll panic.* Without a cell signal, their choices were diminishing. And the car was still popping and fizzing. She didn't want to tell this injured man any of this. Nor did she want to admit that the dog that created this horrific event was hers. The backs of her eyes burned with unshed tears. And that her poor sweet puppy could very well be—

No. Don't go there. Focus on getting this man help.

The man released his seat belt. The only way out for him was to crawl over the passenger seat. But he shouldn't be moving around until a professional looked at him.

"Don't move," she said as he pushed aside the seat belt. "I'll go and get help."

"I'm fine." His voice took on a firm tone.

He was sounding better, but it could just be shock. What if he got out of the car and collapsed in the middle of the road? She certainly couldn't lift him, much less carry him. Even with him being seated, she could see that he was over six feet tall and solidly built. Why did he have to be so stubborn?

The man leaned toward the passenger seat.

"I'm serious. You shouldn't be moving." She swiped her hair out of her face. It was wet from melting snowflakes. It was coming down so hard that she couldn't see much past the other side of the road. "You could make your injuries worse."

As though transforming her concerns into reality, he groaned in pain. Serena's heart lurched. She automatically leaned forward, placing a hand against the man's biceps, helping to support him.

"What is it? What hurts?" Her gaze scanned his body looking for blood or any possible injury, but she didn't spot any.

His breathing was labored. "It's my leg."

"What's wrong with it?"

"I can't move it."

Not good. Not good at all.

And as if matters weren't bad enough, a white cloud billowed out from under the hood. Her heart pounded. What was she supposed to do now?

CHAPTER TWO

SERENA CRAWLED OVER the passenger seat, making her way to the driver's side. "We have to get you out of here. Quickly."

"Don't worry," the man said. "It's just steam."

She wanted to believe him. She really did. But she wasn't sure if the man was totally lucid. For all she knew, he could have a head injury or be in shock or both.

She refused to abandon him. She prayed the car didn't explode into flames before she freed him. With the man slouched over, he was in her way.

With her hand still on his shoulder, she pushed with all her might. He didn't budge. The man was built like a solid rock wall.

"I need you to sit up," she said.

"What?" His voice was a bit groggy. His gaze zeroed in on her. "What are you doing?"

"I need you to move so I can see what's going on with your leg."

"You don't know what you're doing. You're going to make it worse. Go away!"

His harsh words propelled her back out of the car. What was up with this guy? Maybe it was the shock talking.

"I'm trying to help you. Now quit being difficult." She took a calming breath and knelt down again. "Move! Now!"

The man's dark brows rose.

It appeared her brusque words had finally gained his full attention. The man muttered something under his breath. At last, he started to move. He was almost upright when he let out a grunt of pain.

"Is it your leg?"

He nodded as he drew in one deep breath after the other.

She glanced between him and the dash. There just might be enough room for her to wiggle in there. It'd help if she had a flashlight. And then remembering her cell phone, she grabbed it from her pocket and turned on the light.

Her gaze met his. "I'm going to try not to hurt you, but we have to free your leg. Can you work with me on this?"

The man's eyes reflected his uncertainty, but then he relented with a curt nod. "Just do it. And quickly. I smell gas."

He didn't have to tell her twice. On her stomach, she moved across the butter-soft leather upholstery. When she got to the man's body, she did her best to focus on the task at hand and not the fact that when she placed a hand on his thigh, it was rock hard. The man was all muscle and—and she had work to do. At last, she was wedged between him and the dashboard with barely any room for her to move her arms.

"Can you move the seat back?"

His body shifted. "It's not working. The electrical system must have shorted out."

"Okay. I've got this."

She had to get this man free of the car and then find out what had happened to Gizmo. Her poor sweet furbaby could be hurt or worse—

Stop. Deal with one problem at a time.

Hands first, she repositioned herself. She flashed the light around. The side of the car had been smashed inward. His ankle was pinned between the car door and the brake pedal. It looked bad—real bad.

Serena drew in an unsteady breath, willing herself to remain calm when all she wanted to do was run away and find someone else to help this man. But there wasn't time for that. She could do this. She could. Serena placed her hand gently on his leg and paused. When he didn't cry out in pain, she proceeded to examine the situation. She ran her hand down his leg, checking for any major injuries. She didn't feel any. There was no wiggle room on either side. The brake pedal was digging into his flesh.

Knowing that she was going to need two hands, she held up the phone to him. "Can you hold this for me?"

He took the phone. The light was angled too high.

"Tilt it a little lower. I'm going to try to move the brake pedal. Are you ready?"

"Yes. Just do what you need to do."

Serena pressed on the brake. The pedal became stuck on his black leather dress shoe. She tried moving his foot, but it wouldn't budge.

She felt his body stiffen. Serena released his foot. He was really pinned in there. And it frightened her to know that she might not be able to free him before the car went up in flames.

She swallowed hard. "I'm going to take off your shoe and see if that will help."

"Do what you need to do. You don't have to keep updating me."

Just then she inhaled the scent of smoke. Her pulse quickened. They were almost out of time. And this wasn't the way she planned to leave this world.

Her fingers moved quickly. The shoe tie pulled loose.

He cursed under his breath.

She stopped moving. "Sorry."

"Don't be sorry. Keep going."

"But I'm hurting you."

"It's going to hurt a lot more when that fire reaches us."

"Okay. Okay. I've got it. I'll try to do this as quickly as possible."

"Do it!"

The melting snow on the top of her head dripped onto her nose. With her arm, she brushed it off. All her focus needed to be on freeing this man, and in essence herself, from this smashed-up, gasoline-leaking, smoldering car.

Serena once again worked to free his shoe from his foot. It didn't move easily and she suspected he had a lot of swelling going on. She reminded herself to focus on one problem at a time. However, at this moment the problems were mounting faster than she could deal with them.

The smoke caused her to let out a string of coughs.

"Are you okay?" Not even waiting for her answer, he said, "You should get out of here."

"Not without you."

When she moved his foot again, she heard the distinct hiss of his breath. He didn't say anything and so she continued moving his foot. At last, his foot slipped past the brake pedal.

She pulled back. "You're free."

There was perspiration beading on the man's forehead. It definitely wasn't hot in the car. It was more like freezing. Her maneuvering his foot must have hurt him more than he'd let on. She felt really bad adding to his discomfort, but she had no other way to free him.

"Now," she said, "let's get you out of here."

She eased out of the car and attempted to help him, but he brushed her off. The smoke was getting heavier.

"I've got it," he said. "Just move away from the car."

"Not without you." She stood just outside the car.

"Quit saying that. Take care of yourself."

She wasn't backing away. If he needed her, she would be there. The popping and fizzing sounds continued. Her gaze darted to the hood where the smoke was the heaviest. Her attention returned to the man.

Hurry. Please hurry.

She wondered how bad the damage was to his left leg. It suddenly dawned on her that he most likely wouldn't be able to walk on it. But what choice did they have as they were stuck in the middle of nowhere. It was becoming increasingly obvious that no one used this road— at least not in the middle of a snowstorm. And who could blame them, she thought, glancing around at the snow-covered roadway.

Right now, she just wanted to find Gizmo and head back to the cabin. *Gizmo.* Where was he? Her heart clenched with fear. *Please let him be safe.*

It took her assistance to get the man to his feet. Or in his case, his one good foot. He'd finally had to relent and lean on her shoulder. Between hopping and a bit of hobbling, she got him to the other side of the road, a safe distance from the car.

"Thank you," he said. "I don't know what I'd have done if you hadn't come along."

"You're welcome."

"My name's Jackson. What's yours?"

In the daylight, she recognized him. The breath hitched in her throat. He was trouble. Make that trouble with a capital *T* and an exclamation point. He was Jackson Bennett—the god of morning news. She turned away.

He was on the airwaves for three hours each morning in American homes from coast to coast. People quoted him. And quite often his name trended after a particularly stunning interview.

The producers of his show had been in contact with her agent a few times to set up an on-air interview, but each time the logistics hadn't worked for one of them. She couldn't be more grateful about that now. Still, she couldn't breathe. There was a definite possibility that he'd recognize her.

This was not good. Not good at all.

In her mind, he was the enemy—the press. All of her carefully laid plans were in jeopardy. She was surprised he hadn't recognized her already. Would her different hair color and lack of makeup make that much of a difference? She could only hope. After all, who came to the Alps and expected to run across an award-winning movie star from the States?

Regardless, there was no way she was voluntarily outing herself. She'd worked too hard to flee the paparazzi and everything else related to Hollywood, including her agent. It was best that she kept their encounter brief. Not only was she over men, but Jackson was a professional newsman. With enough time, he was bound to sniff out her story.

"Mae. My name's Mae." It wasn't a lie. It was her middle name.

"Mae?" He gazed at her as though studying her face. "You don't look like a Mae."

Oh, no!

"Who do I look like?" The words were out before she could stop them. She wanted to kick herself for indulging in this conversation that had a distinct possibility of blowing up in her face.

He continued to study her. "Hmm... I'll have to give that some thought."

There was a large rock nearby. She brushed off some of the freshly fallen snow. "Sit here and wait. I'll be right back."

"Where are you going?"

Gizmo's name clogged in her throat. She'd never be able to get the words out. She swallowed hard. "I... I have to check on something."

"It's too late to save the car."

She turned to find fire engulfing the hood. If Gizmo was there—if he was trapped—she had to help him. Serena quickly set off for the car, before she could talk herself out of her plan.

Jackson was shouting at her to stop, but she kept going. She would be careful—as careful as she could be. She could feel Jackson's gaze following her. She didn't care what he thought. If Gizmo was hurt and needed her, she had to help him.

Serena rushed through the thickening snow to the car. She carefully made her way down over the small embankment. All the while, she kept an eye out for any sign of her buddy. Between the snow and the wind, there was no sign of his little footprints.

With great trepidation, she turned toward the

place where the car was smashed against the trees. Could he be in there?

She rushed over and bent down. She reached out to sweep away the snow from around the front tire, but for the briefest moment, she hesitated. Her whole body tensed as she imagined the ghastly scene awaiting her.

She gave herself a mental shake. With trembling hands, she set to work. And then at last, most of the snow had been swept away. There was no Gizmo. She took her first full breath. It didn't mean he was safe, but it was a good sign. And right about now, she'd take any positive sign possible.

She turned in a full circle, searching for him. She even ventured the rest of the way down the embankment. There was no sign of him. The crash must have spooked him. How far had he run? And how long would he last in the extreme conditions? She repeatedly called his name.

Between the thickening clouds and the heavy snow, visibility wasn't great. With the deepest, most painful regret, she realized she couldn't help Gizmo. A sob caught in her throat. The backs of her eyes stung. She couldn't fall apart—not yet. She had to get Jackson to safety and then she'd return to continue her search for Gizmo. The car continued to smoke and smolder, so she scooped up some armfuls of snow and heaped them on the hood, hoping to douse the flames. She then moved to the side of the car and, catching sight of a bag in the back seat, she retrieved the large duffel bag.

She returned to the rock where the man was still sitting. "I need to get you out of this weather."

"What were you doing?"

"What are you talking about?"

"Just now. You were searching for something." And then his eyes widened. "That dog. He's yours."

Once more her eyesight blurred with unshed tears. She blinked repeatedly. She nodded.

"It almost killed me." The man's deep voice rumbled.

Serena's chin lifted and her gaze narrowed in on him. "And you might have very well killed him."

As though her pointed words had deflated him, the man had the decency to glance away. His anger immediately dissipated as the gravity of the situation sunk in.

"Are you sure?" he asked. "I tried to miss him."

"I called him and I searched around, but I didn't find any sign of him."

"And just now, when you returned to the car, were you looking under it for your dog?"

She struggled to keep her emotions in check. She nodded. It was the best she could do.

"I'm sorry." His tone softened. "I'd never intentionally hurt an animal."

"It's not your fault. It's mine. I let him off his leash. I should have known better."

"Maybe he's okay. Maybe he got lost."

She shook her head, wishing Jackson would be quiet. He was attempting to comfort her, but it wasn't working. Aside from seeing Gizmo alive and healthy, nothing would soothe her pain and guilt.

She couldn't let herself think about Gizmo any longer. She had to take care of Jackson. And the way he was favoring his leg, there was no way she would be able to get him back to her cabin without a little help. Her cabin was a ways from here. And it was situated in a secluded area. That was why she'd chosen it. It was far from prying eyes and, most important, the press.

But now, well, the location wasn't ideal to obtain medical aid. But she was certain that once she got ahold of the rescue services, they'd send someone to get Jackson medical treatment.

With her thoughts focused on getting help, she turned to Jackson. "I have a place. But I think you're going to need some help getting there."

"I'll make it." He stood upright. He'd barely touched the ground with his injured leg when his face creased with obvious pain.

"Are you ready to concede now?"

His gaze didn't meet hers. "What do you have in mind?"

"I'm going to look for a tree branch that you can use as a cane. Between my shoulder and the tree branch, hopefully we'll be able to limp you back to the cabin."

"Cabin?"

"Uh-huh. Is that a problem?"

"Um. No. I won't be there long."

A smile pulled at her lips at Jackson Bennett's obvious disapproval of staying in a cabin. He had absolutely no idea that it was a two-story log home with just about every creature comfort you could imagine. But Jackson was right about one thing: he wouldn't be staying with her for long. Once she had phone service, he'd be on his way to the hospital and out of her life.

CHAPTER THREE

"ARFF!"

Jackson Bennett glanced around. Was it possible that the dog the woman was so worried about had been unharmed? He hoped so.

He squinted through the heavy falling snow. Where was the dog? Maybe if he caught it, he'd be able to pay the woman back. They could part on even terms. He hated feeling indebted to anyone. If only he could locate the source of the barking.

"Arff! Arff!"

He glanced around for some sign of Mae. Maybe she could find the dog. But it appeared she was still off in search of a makeshift cane for him.

Jackson got to his feet. With difficulty, he turned around. There beneath a tree, where the snow wasn't so deep, stood a little gray-and-white dog. It looked cold and scared. Jackson could sympathize.

"Come here," he said in his most congenial tone. "I won't hurt you."

There was another bark, but it didn't move. The dog continued to stare at Jackson as though trying to decide if Jackson could be trusted or not. Jackson kept calling to the dog, but the little thing wouldn't come near him. Jackson smothered a frustrated sigh. How did he gain the dog's trust?

He again glanced around for Mae. How far had she gone for the walking stick? A town on the other side of the Alps? Italy perhaps?

He considered shouting for her, but then he changed his mind. If he frightened the dog, they'd never catch it. And it wasn't fit for man or beast in this snowstorm.

Jackson turned back to the dog. If only he had a way to coax him over, but he didn't have any dog treats. And then he thought of something. He'd missed his lunch and had grabbed a pack of crackers to eat in the car. Would a dog eat a cracker?

Jackson had no idea. His experience with a dog consisted of exactly seven days. And it hadn't gone well at all.

Once the dog had made a mess on the floor, chewed one of his mother's favorite shoes and howled when his mother put him in the backyard for the night, she'd taken the dog back to the shelter. Jackson remembered how crushed he'd been. He'd begged and pleaded for his mother to change her mind. His mother had told him that it was for the best and sent Jackson to his room.

He banished the memories to the back of his mind. Those days were best forgotten. His life was so much different now—so much better. He didn't have a dog and, for all intents and purposes, he didn't have a mother, either. It was for the best.

He pulled the crackers from his dress shirt pocket. He undid the cellophane and removed one. It consisted of two crackers with cheese spread between them. He hoped this would work.

"Here, boy."

The dog's ears perked up. That had to be a good sign. The pup took a few steps forward. His nose wiggled. Then his tail started to wag.

"That's it. Come on."

The dog's hesitant gaze met his and then returned to the cracker. The pup took a few more steps. He was almost to Jackson.

Jackson lowered his voice. "That's a good boy." He laid the cracker flat on his hand and took a wobbly step forward. The dog watched his every move but held his ground. Jackson stretched out his arm as far as it'd go.

And then the dog came closer. After a few seconds of hesitation, he grabbed the cracker. Jackson caught sight of the blue sparkly collar on the dog's neck. Something told him that this was most definitely the woman's dog. The flashy collar was in line with the woman's rhinestone encrusted cell phone and her perfectly manicured nails.

As the dog devoured the cracker, Jackson knew this was his moment to make his move. Balancing his weight on one foot, he bent down. He lunged forward to wrap his hands around the little dog.

The dog jumped back and Jackson lost his balance. He reached out to regain his balance, but he'd moved too far from the large rock. He instinctively put his weight on his injured leg. Wrong move. He swore under his breath.

"What in the world!" came the beautiful stranger's voice.

It was too late. She couldn't help him. His injured leg couldn't take the pressure of his weight. It gave way. He fell face-first into the snow.

Jackson sat up with snow coating him from head to toe. He blew the snow from his mouth and nose. Then he ran a hand over his face. At that moment, he felt something wet on his cheek. He opened his eyes to find the dog licking him. *Ugh!*

"Aww…you found him." A big smile bloomed on the woman's face. If he thought that she was beautiful before, she was even more of a knock-out when she smiled. "You're such a naughty boy for running off. Come here, Gizmo."

"Gizmo? What kind of name is that?" Jackson attempted to get to his feet. He failed.

The woman's brows drew together, but she didn't move to help him. "What's wrong with his name?"

Jackson sighed. "It's a bit cutesy for a boy, don't you think?"

"Cutesy?" Her green eyes darkened to a shade of deep jade.

"Never mind." What did he care what she named her dog? If his head wasn't pounding, he would have kept his thoughts to himself. He would have to make a mental note to tread carefully going forward. Without Mae's help, he hefted himself to his feet.

In the meantime, she picked up the dog and brushed snow from Gizmo. "We need to get you home and in front of a fire. You poor baby."

As Jackson brushed himself off, he couldn't help but watch how the woman oohed and aahed over the dog. What amazed him the most was how the dog was eating up the attention as though it knew exactly what she was saying.

Mae turned to Jackson as though an afterthought, holding out a stick. "Here you go."

He accepted the sturdy-looking branch. Somehow it made him feel like some sort of Paul Bunyan figure. Although his suit and dress shoes would definitely suggest otherwise.

"How in the world did you find Gizmo?" she asked.

Jackson couldn't actually admit to having done much of anything, but if she wanted to give him partial credit, who was he to reject it. After all, if he hadn't thought of the crackers in his pocket, the dog might have run off again.

"We sort of found each other. And he likes the same crackers as I do."

"Crackers?"

"Yes. I have some in my pocket. They were supposed to replace my lunch, but I got distracted when I turned on the wrong road and my GPS wouldn't work out here. Anyway, I forgot about them."

She nodded as though she understood, but there were still unspoken questions in her eyes. "I hate to say it, but the snow's not letting up. If anything, it's getting heavier." She frowned as she glanced upward. "I threw a bunch of snow on the fire when I was looking for Gizmo. I think it doused it. If not, this heavy snow should take care of it." She turned to him. "Are you ready to hike out of here?"

"I don't see where I have a choice."

"I've got to carry Gizmo because the snow is starting to get too deep for his short legs. And I'll take your bag as you'll need all your energy to move on your good leg. But you can put your arm over my shoulder to balance yourself. Hopefully between that and the cane, you'll be able to make it back to the cabin."

"Sounds like a plan."

He got a firm grip on the stick and placed an arm over her shoulders, trying not to put too much pressure on her. He felt guilty that he couldn't even relieve her of his bag, but she was right, anything more would unbalance him. His ankle was really starting to throb now that the adrenaline was wearing off.

She glanced over at him. "Thank you for finding Gizmo."

"You're welcome."

Were those unshed tears shimmering in her eyes? But in a blink, they were gone. And he wasn't sure if he'd imagined them after all.

At least, they were now even. He glanced over at his snow angel. She was the most beautiful woman he'd ever laid his eyes on. It was hard to miss her stunning green eyes. They were unforgettable and strangely familiar. But that was impossible, right? After all, she was here in Austria and he was from New York City.

But the more he thought about it, he realized that she spoke with an American accent. Now, that he found interesting. What was an American woman doing in Austria at Christmastime? Did she have family here? Or was it something else? Perhaps it was the journalist in him, but he was curious about her story. And then he wondered if she might have an interesting story—something to humanize the holiday segment that he'd flown here to film.

He assured himself that it was professional interest—nothing more. After all, he was off the market. Ever since his wife passed away, he'd kept to himself. No one could ever fill the empty spot in his heart and he had no desire to replace his wife, not now—not ever.

Their progress was slow but steady. He felt bad for holding her back. "Why don't you go on ahead?" he suggested. "You've got to be cold."

"No colder than you. And I'm not leaving you out here. You don't even know where my cabin is."

"I can follow your tracks—"

"No. We're in this together."

Boy, was she stubborn. Even though it irked him that Mae was out here in the frigid air on his account, a small part of him admired her assertiveness. She would certainly be a tough nut to crack during an interview. Those were the interviews he enjoyed the most. The ones where he had to work hard to get the interviewee to open up—to get to the heart of the matter.

A lot of his peers would disagree and say that an interview should flow smoothly. But he wasn't afraid of confrontation—of setting matters straight. But being stuck on the morning news cycle, he didn't get to do many meaty interviews—certainly not as many as he would like.

They continued on in silence. And that was quite all right with Jackson. His head hurt. No, it pounded. But that pain was nothing compared to his ankle. However, he refused to let any of that stop him.

He clenched his jaw as he forced himself to keep moving. It was very slow progress, but one step at a time, he was moving over the snow-laden ground. The snow had seeped into his dress shoes. At first, his feet had grown cold. Then they had begun to hurt. Now they were numb.

He sure hoped they got to their destination soon. Freezing to death might make a big news story—but he wasn't that desperate for headlines.

He glanced once more at Mae, but she'd

pulled up her hood with the fluffy white fur trim, blocking the view of her beautiful face. "Is it much farther?"

"It's just over that rise." She turned her head, sending him a concerned look. "Do you need to rest?"

"No." If he stopped now, he doubted he'd be able to move again. "I can make it."

"Are you sure?" There was a distinct note of doubt in her voice.

"I'm sure." His teeth started to chatter, so he clenched his jaw together.

Attempting to keep his thoughts on anything but the unending cold, he glanced at the woman next to him. He was torn between being angry at her for causing the accident by letting her dog loose and being grateful that she was some sort of angel sent to rescue him.

Then guilt settled in. How could he be upset with someone who was so concerned for him? She may have been irresponsible with the dog, but she'd cared enough to help him. He couldn't forget that. Perhaps this was the twist in the story he'd come to Austria to tell. Perhaps he could attribute her actions to the holiday spirit. Maybe that was stretching things, but he liked the sound of it. He knew that angle would tug on the heartstrings of his viewers. But it wouldn't be enough to garner the attention of the television executives—the same people who had passed him over for the evening news anchor role.

He stared straight ahead. There indeed was a slight hill. In his condition, it seemed more like Mont Blanc. But between the thick tree limb that Mae had located for him and her slim shoulders, he would make it.

Hopefully this cabin came equipped with a landline. He had to get out of here. This wasn't a vacation for him. He was on assignment and his film crew was due to arrive tomorrow. He'd arrived early to scout out some special settings for his Christmas-around-the-world series. This accident would definitely put a crimp in his plans, but by tomorrow he'd be back on track. He refused to let his ankle and various minor injuries hold him back—not when there was work to be done.

He didn't know how much time had passed when the cabin at last came into sight. He paused for a moment, catching his breath. But only for a moment and then he was moving again—pushing through the pain. Between the snow and his injured leg, this walk was a bigger workout than he normally experienced at the gym.

His body was giving in to the cold and he stumbled. "We need to stop."

She narrowed her gaze. "Are you quitting on me? Are you a quitter?"

"I'm not a quitter." What was wrong with her? "Can't you see that I'm injured?"

"I think you're being a wimp."

"Wimp?" He glared at her. Anger warmed his veins. He'd been wrong about her. This woman wasn't an angel—not even close. She was rude and mean.

He'd show her.

He kept going.

One slow, agonizing step after the other.

CHAPTER FOUR

AT LAST.

Serena's gaze zeroed in on the large log cabin. Any other time, she'd stop to admire how picturesque it looked with the snow-covered roof and the icicles hanging around the edges. But not this afternoon. With the thickening snow and the added weight from supporting Jackson, her back ached and her legs were exhausted. Still, her minor discomforts were nothing compared to Jackson's injuries.

She felt bad for being so mean to him back there. But angering him enough for him to prove her wrong was the only way she knew how to keep him going—how to save his life.

If he'd stopped, she'd have never gotten him moving again. Pain and fatigue were deeply etched on his handsome face. And there was no way she was letting her favorite morning news show anchor become a human Popsicle.

Still, she had to temper her sympathy. If she

let herself become too involved with this man, she'd end up paying a steep price. Her last romance had cost her dearly.

Her thoughts turned to Shawn McNolty—Hollywood's rising star. He'd also costarred in Serena's latest movie, which was set to release over the holidays. During the filming, their agents had contrived for them to be seen together to get the public buzzing about a potential romance. But as time went on, Shawn had convinced Serena that instead of putting on a show they could start a genuine romance. He had been so charming and attentive that she'd convinced herself that taking their romance from the big screen to real life could work.

And everything had been all right, or so she'd thought, until she overheard Shawn talking to one of his friends. They'd been out to dinner and she was just returning from the ladies' room while they were standing in the waiting area. Shawn was telling his friend that his arrangement with Serena was working out much better than he'd planned. The longer he spent escorting Serena around town, the more promo he got. The more headlines he received, the more movie scripts came his way. And the best part was Serena didn't even have a clue. He prided himself on being that good of an actor. The memory still stung.

He wasn't the first man to date her in order to further his acting career, but she'd soon realized with those other men that the relationship was one-sided at best. But there was something about Shawn that had caught her off guard. Maybe it was his dark, mysterious eyes or his warm laugh that made her stomach quiver or the way he looked at her like she was the only woman in the world for him. Whatever it was, she'd convinced herself to let go of the past. She'd been sure Shawn was different—that he'd truly cared about her.

Maybe that was why she hadn't suspected something was up when he continually demanded that they go out instead of chilling at her Beverly Hills mansion. He always insisted that they stop and pose for the paparazzi, saying that it was good publicity for their upcoming film. The list of suspicious activities went on—activities that at the time she'd refused to see, but later it had all made sense. The pieces had all fallen into place when she overheard his words at the restaurant. Shawn McNolty had used her for his personal gain.

But he wasn't the only actor in this relationship. Not wanting a public confrontation, she swallowed her heated words and pretended that she hadn't heard a word he'd said about her. Serena didn't even remember what she'd ordered for dinner that last night or how she made it through the meal before she pleaded a headache and took a cab home. The rest of the evening was a blur.

Finding out that her romantic relationship was nothing but a sham was followed by a voice mail from her agent telling her that she'd been turned down for not one but two serious award-contending roles. At that point, she had nothing keeping her in California. She'd needed some downtime. A chance to unplug and regroup. That was the moment when her plan to go off the grid had been born.

With the aid of some temporary hair dye left over from Halloween, she'd switched her honey-blond hair to red. She'd been told by her house-keeper that she was practically unrecognizable without her distinctive eye makeup. Add a ball cap and nondescript jeans, and her disguise had been complete. She'd marched right out the door and jumped in a cab bound for the airport.

And now, even though she had the best of intentions, she knew taking this journalist into her home would end up decimating her serene escape from reality. Jackson may not be on the same level as the paparazzi who would climb the trees outside her Hollywood home, but as soon as he recovered, he'd want something from her—just like Shawn.

Unless she drove Jackson directly to the hospital. It would be what was best for all of them. And her rented all-terrain vehicle was sitting in the driveway. If she could make it to the road, the rest would be slow going, but she was confident she could make it, at least to the nearby village. It may not have a hospital, but there should at least be a doctor. Right?

When they reached the vehicle, she stopped. "Just give me a second."

"What are you doing?"

"Looking for my keys." She pulled off her glove and reached in her coat pocket. Her fingers wrapped around the keys. "Okay. Let's get you seated." She brushed some of the snow from around the door. When she pulled it open, the man sent her a puzzled look. "Come on. We have to get going before the snow gets worse."

His gaze narrowed. "You know how to drive in this much snow?"

Not really. A few times, she'd driven when she was in Tahoe, but it hadn't been in a snowstorm. Still, these weren't normal circumstances.

"I... I've done it before."

He looked at her, then the vehicle and finally at the rise up to the road. He shook his head. "No way. I'll wait here until the authorities can get me."

"But—"

"*Arff! Arff!*"

Gizmo started to wiggle in her arm. "Okay, boy."

"I think he agrees with me. We should go inside."

"We can't." When the man's eyebrows rose, she added, "I mean, you need medical attention."

"I'll be fine. Unless we get in the vehicle and end up in another accident."

She worried her lip. She was out of reasons not to take this journalist into her home. She quickly inventoried the cabin's contents to make sure there wasn't anything lying about that would give away her true identity. There were the contents of her wallet, but he wouldn't see that unless she gave him reason to be suspicious of her—like standing here in the snow, making him wonder why she didn't just take him straight inside.

Serena inwardly groaned.

Stubborn man.

"I know I'm a stranger," he said. "But I promise you no harm."

She wasn't afraid of him. At least, not in the manner that he thought. But at this point, he was either an excellent actor or he hadn't figured out her true identity. Perhaps the hair dye, Strawberry Temptation, and lack of makeup worked as well as her housekeeper had said.

"Arff! Arff!"

She couldn't fight them both. "Well, don't just stand there. Let's go inside."

Serena again let Jackson lean on her shoulder. Trying to get him up the snowy, icy steps was quite a challenge. She wasn't sure her shoulders would ever be the same again. But at last, they made it.

She helped him into the warm cabin and shut the door on the cold. She normally loved snow. But not this much, this fast. And not when it left her snowbound with a member of the press.

She helped him take off his gloves and wool dress coat. He was totally soaked. And ice-cold. His teeth chattered. The only way to warm him up was to strip him down. She started to loosen his tie.

His hand covered hers. "I... I think you're pretty and all, but...but I don't move this fast."

He thought she was coming on to him? She lifted her chin to set him straight when beyond his bluish lips and chattering teeth, she noticed a glint of merriment in his eyes. He was teasing her. That had to be a good sign, right?

"I'm glad to see your sense of humor is still intact, but if you don't get out of these wet clothes, you're going to get severe hypothermia." She attempted to move his hand, but he wouldn't budge.

"I know how to undress myself."

"Fine. Take everything off. I'll get you some blankets." Seeing him standing there leaning all of his weight on his good leg, she knew he was close to falling over from pain and exhaustion. "Let's move you closer to the fire."

She once again lent him her shoulder. Lucky for both of them, the couch was close by. Once he was seated and loosening his tie, she worked on getting a fire started.

A few minutes later, she returned to the great room with her arms piled high with blankets. Jackson sat on the couch in nothing but his blue boxers and socks. Heat immediately rushed to her cheeks. She was being silly. This was an emergency and it wasn't like she was a virgin.

"Something wrong?" he asked.

She knew she was blushing and there was nothing she could do to stop it. She averted her gaze. "Here you go."

She set the blankets beside him. One by one, she draped them over him. That was better. But she couldn't get the image of his very lean, very muscular body out of her mind.

She swallowed hard. "You forgot your socks and they're soaked. I'll get them—"

"No. I can do it." There was obvious weariness in his voice and his eyes drooped closed. "Stop…"

She ignored his protest and set to work. She removed the sock from his good leg. His foot was scary cold. She held it between her hands, trying to get the circulation going. It didn't work.

She glanced up at her unexpected guest. His eyes were still closed. Next, she worked the sock from his injured leg. His ankle was swollen and an angry mess of red and purple bruises.

"Is something the matter?"

His voice startled her. "Um, no." She had to tell him something. "It's just that your feet are so cold."

"They'll be fine."

"It could be frostbite. You weren't exactly dressed to hike through a blizzard. Can you feel your toes? They are awfully pale."

"They have that pins-and-needles sensation."

Holding his feet in her hands wasn't going to be enough help. She grabbed a basin of luke-warm water for him to soak his feet in. He put up a fuss, but eventually he gave in to her ministrations.

When Jackson's feet had sufficiently warmed up, he settled back on the couch. "How does it look?"

The horrible purple-and-red bruise was on both sides of his ankle. The inside wasn't as bad as the outside, but the ankle was a mess. And it was swollen to the point that she couldn't see his ankle bone.

"I think it's broken," she said as though she had any clue about medicine.

"Are you a doctor?" he asked.

"Me? No." Heat swirled in her chest and rushed up to her face. She knew where this conversation was headed.

He arched a brow as he studied her face. "I have the strangest feeling that we've met before. Have we? Met before, that is?"

"No. I don't believe we have."

She knew for a fact that they'd never crossed paths. For the most part, her life was limited to Los Angeles while she knew his work kept him based in New York City. And if they had met, she wouldn't have forgotten. The man was drop-dead gorgeous, and he had the sexiest deep voice. He was the only reason she tuned into the morning news show.

And now he was here, in her cabin, in nothing but his underwear. But it couldn't be further from a romantic interlude. He was a member of the press and she was a Hollywood star in hiding. Once he figured out who she was, he'd broadcast it to the world. The thought made her stomach roil, especially after the mess she'd left behind in California.

"Hmm... I don't know where I've seen you, but I'm good with faces. It'll come to me."

Not if she could help it.

She retrieved a towel that she'd grabbed while gathering the blankets for Jackson. She called Gizmo over and dried him off. Then she situated him on a chair near the fire with an extra blanket. The puppy immediately settled down. With one eye closed and one partially open, he looked at her as though to make sure she didn't go anywhere.

"I won't leave you." She petted him and then kissed the top of his fuzzy head.

She got to her feet and turned to Jackson. "I'll call emergency services. They'll be out in no time to take you to the hospital and deal with your car."

"I'm sorry to be such a bother."

"It was my fault, or rather my dog's. Anyway, everything turned out okay. Except for your ankle...and your car." She moved to the phone on the desk.

When she'd checked in at the leasing office, they'd warned her that cell service was spotty in the mountains so they'd installed a landline. She picked it up and held the cordless phone to her ear. There was no sound. She pressed the power button on and off a few times, but there was still no dial tone. *Great!*

She could only hope she'd get a signal with her cell phone. She hadn't in the couple of days she'd been here, so why would today be any different? But she refused to give up hope.

With her cell phone in hand, she headed for the door. She paused to slip on her boots.

"Where are you going without a coat?" Jackson asked.

"Out on the porch. The phone lines must be down due to the storm, so I'm going to see if I can get a cell signal outside."

He didn't say anything more. She noticed this was the first time she'd headed for the door without Gizmo hot on her heels. Today's adventure had wiped him out. He hadn't budged from the chair. In fact, at one point she'd heard Gizmo snoring. He was so sweet and she felt so blessed that he was safe.

She paced from end to end of the large porch. There was no signal at all. She held it above her head and craned her neck to see if that helped. It didn't.

She lifted on her tiptoes and waved it around. Nothing. She leaned out over the large wooden banister. Snow fell on her phone and her arm, but there was still no signal. There had to be something she could do.

Her gaze moved to her rented all-terrain vehicle. Maybe she could go get help. But then she noticed how the snow was piled up around the tires. She glanced into the distance and she couldn't even see the line of trees at the end of the smallish yard. Who was she kidding? She'd never even get out of the driveway.

With a heavy sigh, she turned back toward the door. Chilled to the bone, she rushed back inside. She brushed the snow from her arm.

"Well?" Jackson's weary voice greeted her.

"Do you want the bad news? Or the bad news?"

He arched a dark brow. "Is that a trick question?"

"Not at all. So which shall it be?"

Was that the beginning of a smile pulling at his lips? Serena couldn't quite be sure. And then she conjured up the image of him smiling like he did each morning on television when he greeted the viewers. He was so devastatingly sexy when he smiled—

"Did you hear me?" Jackson sent her a funny look.

She'd lost track of the conversation, but she knew that he was waiting on her news. "The bad news is that there's no phone service whatsoever."

"And the other bad news?"

"We're stuck here. Together."

His handsome face creased with frown lines.

"And exactly how long do you think we'll be snowbound?"

She shrugged. "Your guess is as good as mine. They did warn me when I rented this place that should there be a snowstorm, it would be quite a while until they dug me out considering I'm off the beaten path."

"Just great." He raked his fingers through his thick brown hair. "I can't be stuck here. I have a job to do."

Did he mean reporting that he'd found her? Serena didn't want to believe he was like the paparazzi. She wanted to believe that Jackson Bennett had integrity and honor. But she couldn't trust him. She couldn't trust anyone—including her own judgment. She always wanted to see the best in people. And that had gotten her into trouble more times than she cared to admit.

Still, she didn't want him to worry. "I promise you that as soon as possible, I'll get you medical attention. And I'm sure soon people will be looking for you."

His eyes widened. "Do you know who I am?"

What was the point in keeping it a secret? "You are Jackson Bennett. You're the face of *Hello America*."

A pleased look came over his face. "And I'm here on assignment. I have a camera crew flying in to help me film some Christmas segments."

It was on the tip of her tongue to ask him if she was to be included in one of those segments, but she caught herself just in time. If he could be believed, he didn't recognize her. "I can promise you, they aren't getting through the storm."

"Is it getting worse?"

She nodded.

He muttered under his breath. "I can't just sit here."

He went to stand up. As soon as his injured foot touched the ground, his face reflected the pain he felt.

"Sit back down. First, I think I should bandage your ankle and then you can sleep. When you wake up, help should be here." She sincerely hoped so, for both of their sakes.

This luxury cabin may come with a fully stocked pantry and fridge, but something told her it would be lacking on first-aid items. She'd have to be inventive.

CHAPTER FIVE

JACKSON BLINKED.

It took him a moment to gain his bearings. That hike had taken more out of him than he'd expected. After Mae had bandaged his ankle, she'd helped him into a pair of sweatpants and a long-sleeved T-shirt he'd packed in his bag, her cheeks pinking prettily all the while, and settled him on the couch with pillows and blankets. She'd then insisted that he get some rest.

As time went by, there were very few spots on his body that didn't hurt. He didn't want to think of what would have happened to him if it wasn't for Mae. The mental image of his car going up in flames sent cold fingers of apprehension trailing down his spine.

Mae tried to act tough, but he'd watched how she fussed over her dog. She was a softy on the inside. In fact, he was willing to bet there was a whole lot more to Mae than being an angel of mercy. So what exactly was her story?

And what was she doing in this isolated cabin?

Jackson's gaze followed the stone chimney of the fireplace up, up and up until he reached the impressive cathedral ceiling. He took in the balcony and could only imagine what the second story must be like. Okay, this place was much more than a cabin. It was a luxury log home at the least and more like a mansion.

Was Mae staying here all by herself?

The place was much too big for just one person. Oh, and her dog. How could he forget Gizmo? She'd be lucky if the dog didn't get lost in here.

He gave himself a mental shake to clear his thoughts. He had a lot more important things to worry about than this woman's extravagance. He had to find a way to salvage his career—his stagnant career.

Ever since his wife passed away, his job was what got him up in the morning and helped him through the days. The nights were a different matter. He was left with nothing but memories of the only woman that he would ever love. When she'd died, he didn't know how he'd go on. In the beginning, breathing had taken effort. His existence had been an hour-to-hour proposition. And then he'd progressed to day by day. That was when he'd sought refuge in his work—going above and beyond for a good story.

His work was the sole reason he was in Austria. It was the second Christmas since he'd lost his wife, and he couldn't stay in New York City. He didn't want to be invited to friends' holiday celebrations. He didn't want tickets to Christmas programs in theatres. He wanted to be alone, but no one seemed to understand.

He may not be able to totally escape the holiday, but at least in Austria it would be on his terms. Jackson took in the towering pine tree in front of the two-story windows. And when his gaze landed on the boxes of decorations, he realized that he'd been taken in by a Christmas zealot. He sighed. This was just his luck. The sooner he got out of there, the better.

Speaking of his beautiful hostess, where had she gone? He paused and listened. Nothing. Was she napping? If so, he couldn't blame her. The afternoon had been horrific and stressful, not to mention the hike over mountainous terrain with him hanging on her shoulder. He'd tried not to lean on her too much, but at times, she was the only thing keeping him from falling face-first in the mounting snow.

He glanced to the spot where the dog had been lying on a blanket. Even he was gone. That was strange. He was just there a moment ago—right before Jackson had closed his eyes to rest them.

Jackson decided it was best that he go check on things. He saw his makeshift cane close by and grabbed it. His gaze moved to his bandaged ankle. He'd be lucky if it wasn't broken, but he wasn't going to think about that now.

With a firm grip on the cane, he lifted himself up on his good leg. What he wouldn't give now for a set of crutches. He turned himself around, finding the cabin even larger than he'd originally imagined. This place could easily fit three or four families.

Just then Mae appeared with her arms full of clothes. "What are you doing up?"

"I was wondering where you'd slipped off to."

"Well, when you fell asleep, I decided I should move my things out of the master suite to one of the upstairs rooms."

"Upstairs? But why? I'll be out of here in no time."

Mae moved to an armchair and laid her clothes across the back of it. "About that, I don't think either of us is going anywhere anytime soon."

"What? But why?"

"The snow hasn't stopped."

He half hopped, half limped his way to the door and looked out. The sun was setting, not that it was visible with the snow clouds blanketing the sky. But evening was definitely settling in. And Mae was right. The snow, if anything, had gotten worse. There were several new inches out there since they'd arrived at the cabin.

"It doesn't look good," he grudgingly conceded.

"Don't worry. I have plenty of food."

She might be sure of that fact, but he wasn't. It wasn't like they were in a cabin in a highly populated ski resort. This place was miles from the closest village, and from what he could tell, there were no neighbors close by.

He settled on the edge of the couch. "Um, thanks." He wasn't sure what else to say. "But I don't want to put you out. I can take the room upstairs."

From across the room, she sent him an I-don't-believe-you look. "On that leg? I don't think so." She started to pick up the clothes again. "I have dinner under control."

Come to think of it, he was hungry. Jackson sniffed the air, but he didn't smell anything. "What is it?"

"I hope chili will do."

Chili sounded good on such a cold evening. "Sounds great. Do you need help in the kitchen?"

She shook her head. "There's nothing to do but open a couple of cans and warm them up."

Open cans? Was she serious? He did his best

to eat healthy. When your career involved standing before the cameras—cameras that picked up every shadow and wrinkle—you learned to drink lots of water and avoid food out of a can.

"Is that a problem?" her voice drew him from his thoughts.

"No. Thanks for taking me in and feeding me. I will pay you back."

She shook her head. "That's not necessary."

She had a point. Anyone who could afford a place this extravagant didn't need a handout. Far from it.

"Are you staying in this massive log home by yourself?" He vocalized his thoughts before he could register how that might sound.

Her brows arched. "I am." She paused as though trying to decide what to say next. "It's all they had left when I arrived."

So this trip was spur-of-the-moment. He found that interesting. To his surprise, he was finding most everything about this woman interesting. That hadn't happened to him since… since he'd met his wife.

Not that his interest in Mae was remotely similar to the way he felt about June. He supposed that it was only natural to feel some sort of indebtedness to the person who saved your life. That had to be it. For all he knew, he'd hit his head in the accident. It sure hurt enough to have struck something.

"Sorry. I didn't mean to be nosy," he said. "I guess it's just the nature of my job."

Just then Gizmo came running into the room.

"Gizmo, stop." Mae had a horrified look on her face.

Jackson couldn't help but wonder what had put that look on her face until the little dog stopped in front of him with something pink hanging from its mouth.

"Gizmo!" Mae rushed forward.

The dog dropped a pink lacy bra at Jackson's feet. He glanced up to find Mae's face the same shade as the delicate bra. Jackson couldn't help himself. On one leg, he carefully maneuvered himself closer to the floor so he could pick up the piece of lingerie.

He straightened just as Mae reached him. A smile pulled at his lips as he held out the bra. "I believe this is yours."

"Quit smiling." She snatched the very alluring bra from him. "It isn't funny."

"Your dog has an interesting sense of humor."

"He's a klepto. That's all." And then realizing that she was still holding the bra in front of him, she moved it behind her back.

"You have good taste." He knew he shouldn't have said it, but he couldn't resist a bit of teasing.

The color heightened in her face. "If you're done critiquing my lingerie, I'll take my clothes upstairs."

She turned promptly. With her head held high and her shoulders rigid, she moved to the armchair. For some reason, he didn't think she would be so easily embarrassed. After all, earlier today she was not afraid to call the shots, including stripping him down to his boxers and then dressing him. But just now, he'd witnessed a vulnerable side of her. *Most intriguing.*

"Pink looks good on you," he called out.

She turned and gave him a dirty look. It was at that point that he burst out laughing. In that moment, he forgot about all his aches and pains. He couldn't remember the last time he'd laughed without it being on cue. It felt good. Real good.

Mae gathered her clothes and strode over to the steps leading to the second floor. A smile lingered on his face as he settled back on the couch. He figured he'd be less of a bother here as opposed to anywhere else.

Gizmo returned to the room. He hefted himself onto the couch. He settled against Jackson's thigh and put his head down. Jackson never bothered with dogs, but maybe Gizmo wasn't so bad after all. He ran his hand over the dog's soft fur. At least, Gizmo had a sense of humor. Unlike his human counterpart.

* * *

This was not the quiet solitude that she'd imagined.

Serena busied herself in the kitchen, trying to put together dinner. But all the while, her thoughts were on Jackson. He was not what she'd expected. He was more down-to-earth. And his eyes, they were—dare she say it— dreamy. She could get lost in them. And his laugh, it was deep and rich like dark French roast coffee.

Realizing that she was in dangerous territory, she halted her thoughts. Maybe she had fantasized about him being the perfect man one too many times while watching his morning show. And now that he was here in her cabin, she was having a hard time separating fantasy from reality.

And her reality right now was preparing an acceptable dinner. For someone who spent very little time in the kitchen because of a constant string of diets, she was pretty pleased with the appearance of dinner. Even Jackson couldn't complain. She hoped…

She glanced down at his tray to make sure she hadn't missed anything. There was a freshly warmed bowl of chili straight out of the can. A spoon and napkin. A glass of water because she didn't know what he liked to drink. But there was something missing. A man his size that had been through so much that day would have a big appetite. Should she add a salad? Nah, it would take too long. And then she decided to add some buttered bread.

When it was all arranged on the tray, she turned toward the door. She just hoped he still had his leg propped up on a pillow. If she could get him moved to the bedroom, she wouldn't have to trip over him in the living room. And maybe then she'd be able to get back to the quiet time so she could do some more work on her screenplay.

Since she'd arrived in Austria, the words had been flowing. Well, maybe not flowing, but they'd been coming in spurts. Sometimes those spurts consisted of an entire scene or two. But other times, she struggled to write a sentence, much less a paragraph. She wondered if that was how it worked for all writers or if it was just because this was her first script.

Serena paused at the doorway. Recalling her monthly indulgence of visiting the local drive-through for a bowl of chili, she realized they would top the bowl with diced onion and cheese. Perhaps she should do the same. The chili did look a little blah. Serena returned to the kitchen island.

By the time she chopped up the onion, her

eyes were misty. Maybe the onion wasn't the best idea, but she wasn't wasting it, so she tossed it on. And then she topped it off with a handful of sharp cheddar. She returned the remaining onion and cheese to the fridge. It was then she noticed some fresh parsley.

Gizmo strolled into the kitchen. He came right up to her. He still had a sleepy look on his face.

She knelt down to fuss over him. Her fingers ran over his downy soft fur. "Hey, sleepyhead, you finally woke up."

"Arff!"

She loved the fact that he spoke to her as though he actually understood what she was saying to him. Sometimes she wondered if he understood more than they said dogs could understand. It was almost as though he could read her mind.

Serena washed her hands before rinsing off the parsley. Then she began to chop it up. She glanced over to find Gizmo lying in front of the stove with his head tilted to the side and staring at her.

"What are you looking at?"

"Arff! Arff!"

"I'm not making a big deal out of this. I would do this for anyone who was injured and needed my help." It didn't matter that Jackson was drop-dead gorgeous and when he laughed, he made her stomach dip like she was on a roller coaster.

She assured herself that she wasn't going out of her way to impress Jackson. She wouldn't do that. After all, she was Serena Winston. Daughter of two Hollywood legends. Heiress to the Winston fortune and an award-winning actress. She didn't need to work to impress any man.

Except that Jackson didn't have a clue who she was. That should be a relief, but it made her wonder if she wasn't pretty without her normal layer of makeup. Or perhaps the strawberry blonde hair didn't work for her. Maybe it was true what they said about blondes having more fun.

What was she doing? She yanked her thoughts to a stop.

Now, because she liked the looks of the parsley and not because she was trying to impress the influential reporter, she sprinkled it over the bowl.

She caught Gizmo continuing to stare at her with those dark brown eyes. "Would you stop looking at me like that?"

Gizmo whined, stretched out on the rug and put his head down. That was better.

Serena again grabbed the tray and headed for

the door. Time to go wait on Jackson. She assured herself that no matter if he smiled at her or not, she would drop off the food and leave. After all, he was enemy number one—the press.

CHAPTER SIX

HE WAS SO comfortable—so relaxed.

And, best of all, he was no longer alone.

Mae was right there, next to him. So close. So temptingly close that he could smell her sexy and flirty perfume. It was the perfect mix of spice and floral scents. As though it had cast a spell over him, he gazed deep into her eyes.

He reached out, pulling her toward him. He ached to feel her lips pressed to his. There was just something about her—about her strawberry blonde hair that turned him on.

"Jackson," she called out to him.

He loved the way she said his name. It was all soft and sultry. He moaned in eager anticipation of where this evening was going to go.

"Jackson."

"Mae." He couldn't bring himself to say more. Why waste time on words when he could show her exactly how he was feeling—

Suddenly, he was jostled.

"Hey, Jackson. Wake up."

His eyes flew open. The bright light from the lamp on the end table caused him to blink. Wait. What was she doing standing there with a tray of food? They had just been snuggled together on the couch.

He blinked, trying to make sense of everything. And then it all came crashing in on him. He'd dozed off again. Fragmented images of his dream came rushing back to him. Not only had he been dreaming, but he'd been dreaming about Mae. He uttered a groan.

A worried look came over her face. "What's the matter? Is it your ankle?"

He hurried to subdue his frustration. What was wrong with him? He had absolutely no interest in Mae. None whatsoever!

He glanced up at her. The look on her face said that with each passing moment she was becoming more concerned about him. What did he say? His still half-asleep mind struggled to find the right words.

"Um… I just moved the wrong way. It's no big deal."

She consulted the clock on the mantel. "You can have some more painkillers. I'll go get you a couple."

Mae set the tray down on the coffee table and rushed out of the room. He didn't argue, because he needed a moment or two to pull himself together. He shifted until he was sitting sideways on the couch, keeping his foot propped up. Realizing he hadn't eaten since breakfast, he reached for the plate of bread.

At that moment, there was a shuffling sound. And then a fuzzy head popped up over the edge of the couch. Without invitation, Gizmo hopped up on the couch. This time he didn't immediately settle down for a nap. His tail swished back and forth.

So the little guy wanted to make friends? Jackson smiled. It'd been a long time since he'd briefly had a dog. And nowadays, his life wasn't conducive to keeping a pet. But that didn't mean he and Gizmo couldn't be friends.

He sat still as the dog paused and sniffed the bandage on his leg. And then the pup continued up the edge of the couch. Jackson was all ready to pet him when the dog became distracted by the food. Before Jackson could move the plate, Gizmo snatched a slice of buttered bread. For a dog with short legs, he sure could move swiftly.

"Hey. Stop."

Gizmo didn't slow down. He jumped off the couch. Just as Mae returned, Gizmo rushed past her. The dog was a blur of gray-and-white fur.

A frown settled on Mae's face. "What did you do to Gizmo?"

"Me?" Jackson pressed a hand to his chest. "Why do you think I did anything?"

"Because I know you don't really like him."

He didn't like Gizmo? Was that really how he came across? Maybe that was why the dog chose the bread over him. The thought didn't sit well with Jackson. He would have to try harder with the little guy—even if he was a bread thief.

Mae crossed her arms, waiting for an answer to her question.

Jackson's gaze met her accusing stare. "I promise you that I didn't do anything to him."

"Then why was he running out of here?"

Obviously she'd missed the piece of bread hanging from the little guy's mouth. Well, who was he to rat Gizmo out? It wasn't like it was going to score him any points with his very protective owner.

"I don't know. Maybe he heard something." Jackson shrugged. And then he held up three fingers. "Scout's honor."

Her stance eased. "You were a Boy Scout?"

"I was." He studied her, surprised by the glint of approval in her eyes. "I take it you approve?"

"I… I guess. I'm just surprised, is all."

For that moment, he wanted to gain her approval. "I was in the Scouts for a number of years."

"You must have enjoyed it."

"I don't know about that. Some of it, sure. But as I got older, I wasn't that into it. But my mother, she insisted I remain a member."

"Your mother? But why?" And then Mae pressed her lips together as though she hadn't meant to utter that question. "Sorry. You don't have to answer that."

He didn't normally open up to people about his past. He glossed over the important parts and left everything else unsaid. But for some reason, he felt like he could open up to Mae. "I was just six when my parents divorced. My father moved on, remarried and had another family. And so he wasn't around much. My mother felt that I needed a male role model. She worried that she wasn't enough for me. And so she enrolled me in Scouts so I could learn to whittle wood and make campfires. You know, all of the stuff that turns a boy into a strong, responsible adult." Now, it was time to turn the tables on her. "And were you a Girl Scout?"

She shook her head. "My, um, parents, they weren't much into me taking part in group functions."

He arched a brow. "I thought all parents wanted their kids to interact with others."

Mae glanced down. "They...they were overprotective."

"Oh. I see. Well, it appears you didn't miss

out on anything by not learning how to build a fire. And think of all the calories you saved by not eating all those s'mores and roasted marsh-mallows."

He was attempting to make her smile, but she was still avoiding his gaze and she definitely wasn't smiling. There was more to her child-hood than she was willing to share. Something told him she hadn't had it easy—even if this luxury log home said otherwise.

"You better eat before it's cold," Mae said.

"What about you? Where's your food?"

"Oh, I'll eat in the kitchen." Her gaze strayed across the plate on his lap. "I see you already ate some of the bread."

"I guess I was hungrier than I thought. Thanks for this."

"It's no big deal. I'm sure your wife did things like this for you all of the time."

"Actually, she didn't. She came from old money and never learned to cook. By the time we met, she had her life the way she wanted it, and so for us to work, I had to fit into her life."

Mae's mouth gaped and then as though catch-ing herself, she quickly forced her jaw closed.

"I see I surprised you with that admission." He sighed. "I guess I surprised myself in a way. My mother was a lot like my late wife. She had her life and I had to fit into it—but I didn't do a very good job. I always thought when I grew up that I would end up with someone who was the exact opposite of my mother. And I convinced myself that June was different. After all, she had money. She didn't need mine. And she was cultured. My mother was anything but cultured." Why was he rambling on? He never opened up about his private life with anyone. "But you don't want to hear all of that."

"Actually, it's nice to know that my life isn't the only one that isn't picture-perfect."

So he was right. She had skeletons in her closet. He wondered what they might be, but he didn't venture to ask. They'd shared enough for one evening.

His steady gaze met hers. "You've been great. I don't know what I'd have done without you. I won't forget it."

Her cheeks filled with color. "It's not that big of a deal."

"I promise that I'll find a way to pay you back." When she went to protest, he said, "I was thinking that once I'm mobile I could treat you to dinner in the village."

This time her gaze did meet his. "I… I don't think that would be a good idea."

Okay. He may have been out of the dating scene for a number of years, but he was pretty sure that wasn't how the conversation was supposed to have gone. Perhaps he hadn't stated it properly.

"I know this place is really nice, but you can't spend all of your time here alone. And I'll be staying in the area until after Christmas, so I'd like to pay you back in some manner. I just thought a friendly dinner might be nice. If you change your mind before I leave tomorrow, I'll give you my phone number."

There, that was much clearer. Surely she wouldn't object now. Would she?

"Thank you." She sent him a small smile. "That's a really nice offer, but you don't have to feel like you owe me anything. After all, if it wasn't for Gizmo, we wouldn't be here."

She did have a point, but he had a feeling she was just using that as an excuse. Did she really find him that repulsive? He wasn't used to a woman rejecting his offer for dinner—not that he dated, but he did have business dinners and he was never without female companionship for those.

Mae was different. Very different. And that made him all the more curious about her. If only they had phone reception, he'd do an internet search on her. After all, he was a reporter. Research was a part of his daily routine. Sure, he had people to do it, but he liked to do a lot of his own research. He liked learning all sorts of new things.

There was only one problem. He didn't know her last name. Was that just an oversight on her part? Or had she purposely withheld it?

"Well, I'll let you eat. I need to go check on Gizmo. He's being suspiciously quiet." She turned to walk away.

"Hey, you never said what your last name is."

"I didn't, huh?" And with that she continued toward the kitchen.

He was staying with a mystery woman who had no lack of funds but guarded her privacy above all else. What had happened to make her so secretive? Or had she always been that way?

The bed started to vibrate.

Serena's eyes opened to find that morning was upon them. But for the life of her, she couldn't figure out what was causing the vibration and it was getting stronger. Was it an earthquake?

Gizmo started to whine. She couldn't blame him. She was used to earthquakes, or rather she was as used to them as you could be when you were a California native. The truth was they always put her on edge. But she hadn't expected to encounter them in Austria. Unless this was something else entirely. Whatever was happening, it wasn't good.

She hugged Gizmo close. "It's okay, buddy. We'll be okay."

Serena scrambled out of bed. She threw on her fuzzy purple robe and headed out the door. Her feet barely touched the staircase.

By the time she reached the first floor, the vibration had stopped. She found Jackson out of bed. He wasn't wearing a shirt, giving her an ample view of his bare back with his broad shoulders and tapered waist. A pair of navy pajama bottoms completed the sexy look. She mentally urged him to turn around.

Instead, he remained with his back to her. His hand was gripped firmly to his makeshift cane as he gazed out the window next to the front door.

Perhaps he hadn't heard her enter the room. "What was that?"

He at last turned, giving her a full view of his muscular chest with a splattering of hair. "I'm not sure, but I'd hazard a guess that it was an avalanche."

Realizing that she was staring at his impressive six-pack abs, she forced her gaze to meet his. "That...that was way too close for my comfort."

"Mine, too," Jackson said matter-of-factly.

She was impressed that he was willing to make such a confession. In her experience, men never admitted to a weakness—least of all her ex-boyfriend. Men were all about putting on a show of how macho they were.

And somehow she'd imagined Jackson, with his bigger-than-life personality, to be full of bravado. Instead, she found him relatable. In that moment, she liked him a little bit more—probably more than was wise considering his means of making a living.

"How far away do you think it was?" she asked, trying to keep her attention on something besides Jackson's temping, naked chest.

"I don't know. The power is out, too."

"Don't worry, we have a generator. The realty people showed me how it works."

He glanced down at his leg. "I'd like to get out there and take a look around, but I'm not as mobile as I'd like to be."

"Speaking of which, you should be in that bed, resting your leg."

He shook his head. "I was going stir-crazy."

"I take it you're not one to sit around."

"Only if I'm doing research for a news story. But seeing as how there's no internet and no phone service, that idea is out."

She was thanking her lucky stars for the lack of communication with the outside world. "I'm sure we'll be able to get you out of here today. Your first stop should be the doctor's or the hospital to have your leg checked."

Jackson glanced back out the window. "The snow is getting lighter, but there's got to be at least three feet of it out there. If not more."

"What?" It wasn't nearly that bad when she'd taken Gizmo outside last night, but it was more than her pampered pooch could appreciate. He definitely enjoyed his California sunshine. But then again, a lot of hours had passed since then.

Serena rushed over to the window to have a look. Jackson wasn't exaggerating. There were no signs of their footsteps from the prior evening. Between the snow and wind, any trace of them had been swept away.

She turned back to Jackson to find him staring at her instead of the snow. Heat swirled in her chest. She was used to having men stare at her, so why was she having such a reaction to Jackson looking at her now?

And then she realized that in her hurry to find out what had caused the massive tremors, she'd rushed downstairs without running a brush through her hair. Unlike his sexy appearance, she must look quite a mess.

How did men wake up looking good? It was frustrating because her hair was always going in far too many directions and sticking straight out in other places. And then she started to wonder if she had drool in the corners of her mouth. A groan started deep inside, but she stifled it. But the heat rushing to her face was unstoppable.

Just then Gizmo moved to the door and started to bark. She made a point of turning away from Jackson as though to talk to the dog. With one hand, she petted Gizmo. With the other hand, she ran her fingers around her mouth. She finally breathed a little easier.

"It's okay, boy. I'll take you out in a minute."

"Out? Where?"

"Lucky for me this cabin is fully prepared for anything. There's a snow shovel on the side of the porch."

Serena dressed quickly and then fired up the generator. She stuffed her feet in a pair of snow boots that she'd picked up in the nearby village upon hearing the forecast. And then she put on her coat and pulled a white knit cap over her mussed-up hair.

After attaching Gizmo's leash, she turned back to Jackson. "After I take him out and shovel for a bit, I'll get you some breakfast."

"You don't have to."

She shrugged. "I'm going to need some breakfast after I shovel out the driveway. Or at least start on it. Suddenly that driveway looks very long."

Jackson's face creased with frown lines. "You shouldn't do all of that shoveling."

"Really? I don't see anyone else around here to help dig us out."

A distinct frown formed on his handsome face. "I should be doing it."

"And how exactly would you manage to shovel snow on one leg?"

"Maybe the sun will melt it."

"When? A month from now?"

He sighed. "Okay. I'll help you."

"No, you won't." She glared at him, hoping he'd understand her level of seriousness. "You'll stay right here."

Not about to continue this pointless argument, she let herself out the door. The snow was light but the wind was still gusting. She could imagine that many of the mountain roads would be impassable and she didn't even want to think of how the avalanche would delay Jackson's departure.

At least if she got the vehicle and the driveway dug out, once the roads were opened, she could get him to the village. She just had to hope that would happen sometime today. The longer they spent together, the harder it was to keep her true identity a secret.

CHAPTER SEVEN

He felt like a caged tiger.

Moving between the window and the couch was making his ankle throb. His conscience wouldn't allow him any peace. He shouldn't be inside this cozy cabin while Mae was outside doing all of the hard work. He felt awful. He'd never had a woman take care of him—not even his wife.

When he'd first met June, she'd been a model and he'd been at the fashion show to do an interview. It was back when he just did spotlight interviews for an evening entertainment show. She was delicate and spoke with a soft voice. She was kind and thoughtful—the exact opposite of his mother.

And in no time, he'd fallen for her. In just a few short months, they'd been married amid her family's protests. With both of them driven by their passion for life and work, their futures were on the rise. Fueled by his determination and June's encouragement, he'd taken on the anchor chair of *Hello America* within six months of their marriage. It appeared that nothing could stop them.

And then a few years later, she'd received the life-altering diagnosis—she had cancer. He clearly remembered that day at the doctor's office with an overhead light flickering, the slight sent of antiseptic in the air and June's muffled cry. Jackson's gut knotted as the memories washed over him. That day was when all their dreams and plans had fallen to the white tiled floor and shattered into a million sharp, jagged pieces.

He'd dropped everything as they'd embarked on the fight of their lives. He'd needed to make sure she was always taken care of, whether it be surgery, a treatment or just being at home recovering from the side effects of her treatments. He'd turned his life upside down and inside out—not because he had to but rather because he wanted to be there for June.

He had her favorite magazines on hand for her to thumb through, her favorite flavored water, chicken broth and movies. He'd never minded. He would have done anything for her. Just the memory of everything she'd endured because of that horrible disease made his stomach turn.

And as much as he'd loved June, he could

see now that she was so different from Mae. June never would have waited on him like Mae had the night before. But that was not exactly fair. Because June didn't know how to cook, she would have called for delivery service.

As for shoveling snow, June hadn't believed in physical labor. It was the way she'd been raised, with a silver spoon in her mouth. And as luxurious as this cabin may be, June wouldn't have voluntarily come here. She liked touring the small villages, but she preferred staying in the city or at the ski resorts. He'd never had a problem with her choices because when she had been happy, he'd been happy.

But maybe there was more to life. A different way of being. Maybe happiness didn't have to be a one-sided venture. A bit of give-and-take sounded appealing—

Stop! What was he going on about this for? It wasn't like he would ever see Mae and her glorious strawberry blonde hair after he got away from here. It still bothered him that he couldn't place her face. You'd think that a knockout like Mae would stick out in his memory. Maybe it was the accident. He didn't say anything to Mae because he didn't want to worry her, but that had to be the source of his headaches and his fascination with her.

In the three years, five months and eleven

days that he'd been with June, he'd never willed her to be anything other than what she was—the woman that loved him. When she'd looked at him, the love had shone in her eyes. No one had ever looked at him that way. Their relationship may not have been perfect, but they'd found a way to make it work.

He jerked his thoughts to a halt. What was the matter with him? Why was he comparing June to Mae?

While Mae was nothing like June, there was something about her—a vulnerability that drew him near. She'd been wounded in the past and was leery of trusting him. They had that in common—the lack of trust. After having loved with all his heart and losing June so quickly, he was wary of letting anyone get close to him. Until now, he hadn't given much thought to how he kept people at arm's length. Maybe it was something they both needed to work on.

Jackson made his way to the kitchen. He may not be any help outside, but he could still whip up a mean breakfast. He pulled open the fridge door to find the shelves loaded with food. Wow! This place was certainly well stocked, or else his beautiful hostess had bought a lot of food for just herself and her dog.

Leaning on one leg tired him quickly, but he refused to give in. He would have a lovely meal ready for Mae. She deserved it. He just wished it would ease his guilty conscience, but preparing breakfast with bacon, eggs, hash browns and pancakes did not even come close to the task of shoveling all that snow.

But thanks to Mae's efforts, he'd soon be getting out of here. The storm was almost over and the road would be opened. And none too soon because he still had to film the segments for the holiday special. He had no idea where his crew was, but they were resilient. He was certain they would have hunkered down for the storm. And as soon as the cell phone service was reestablished, they'd make contact.

However, the holiday special was bothering him. He was better than puff pieces. He wanted to do more substantial segments—the type of investigative reporting that they featured on the evening news. But before he could do that, he had to get a story that would grab the network bigwigs' attention.

He thought of the avalanche. That was a story, but without something more like hikers or skiers trapped, it wouldn't go anywhere. Instead of playing where-in-the-world-is-Jackson? he needed to be tracking down a headline-making story—

"What smells so good?"

He turned from his place at the stove to find

Mae standing in the doorway. But she was frowning, not smiling like he'd envisioned. "What's the matter? Did you hurt yourself?"

"The problem is you. You shouldn't be in here hobbling around."

"I figured you'd work up an appetite."

"I told you I would make food when I came inside."

"And I thought I would surprise you. So... surprise." He grinned brightly, hoping to lighten the mood.

And still there was no smile on her face. It bothered him because she was so gorgeous when she smiled. He remembered how hard it used to be to make June smile when she got in one of her moods. But he'd always persevered until he won out and eventually June would smile at him. Because when he'd said his wedding vows, he'd meant every single word. He would not get a divorce like his parents. He would not fail.

But Mae was not June. Why should he care if she smiled or not?

"Go sit down. I'll finish this," she said.

"It's done. I just have to put this last pancake on the plate. By the way, your fridge was well stocked. I hope you don't mind that I helped myself."

She washed up and then followed him to the kitchen table. "No. I was worried that it would all go bad. So thanks for helping me to put it to good use."

Once they were seated at the table next to a bank of windows, Mae's gaze skimmed over all the serving dishes heaped with food. "Who's going to eat all of this?"

"Arff! Arff!"

They both laughed at Gizmo's quick response.

"It appears that Gizmo worked up an appetite, too," Jackson said.

"I don't know how that could be when he spent the entire time sitting on the porch. He refused to get off it, even after I shoveled out an area in the yard just for him."

Gizmo yawned and whined at the same time.

They both smiled at the animated pooch. Maybe Gizmo wasn't so bad—at least when he wasn't running loose and causing car accidents.

As they each filled their plate, Mae asked, "So what had you so distracted when I walked in?"

"Distracted?" It took him a moment to recall what she was talking about.

"You had a very serious look on your face."

"Oh, I was thinking about work."

"Aren't you supposed to relax? Isn't this a vacation?"

He shook his head. "I came here to work."

Was it his imagination or did Mae's face visibly drain of color. "Um, what's your assignment?" And then as though she realized that she might be prying, she said, "Sorry. I don't mean to be pushy."

"It's okay. I'm doing a Christmas special. You know, a sort of Christmas around the world. I already did one in Ireland, Japan and now Austria. Well, that depends on if I ever find my camera crew after this storm." He glanced out the window. "Hey, the snow is just flurries now."

"That's good, because let me tell you, there's a ton of snow out there." She sighed. "You know, I've worked up such an appetite that I could eat all of this food."

"Go ahead."

She shook her head. "I can't."

"Sure you can. In fact, I can make more."

"Don't tempt me. But really, I can't."

"Don't tell me that you're dieting."

She shrugged. "Okay. I won't tell you."

"What does someone as beautiful as you have to diet for?" He wanted to tell her that she could stand to put on a few pounds, but he didn't dare. He didn't want her to take it the wrong way.

"So I fit in my clothes. But I think I can squeeze in a little more after that exercise this morning." Her gaze met his. "You're a really good cook."

He continued to stare into her green eyes. "I've had a lot of experience."

He didn't bother to add that after his parents divorced, his mother wasn't around much as she had to bounce between two and sometimes three jobs to make ends meet. And so he did the bulk of the cooking. And then with June, she didn't know how to cook and so he'd taken on the role as he enjoyed creating delicious meals that were healthy and nutritious.

"If your job on television ever falls through, you could become a chef."

He smiled at the compliment. "Thanks. I'll keep that in mind. It might come in handy."

Now what was she supposed to do?

Serena stared out the window at the snowy landscape. They still hadn't plowed open the road and there was no way that she could drive through three feet plus of snow. She would have to have a monster truck with chains on the tires and even then she doubted that she'd make it out of the driveway.

With a heavy sigh, she accepted that there was nothing she could do for now. Instead of wasting her energy worrying about Jackson's presence, she needed to concentrate on writing a screenplay.

This was her chance to make a name for herself that had nothing to do with her looks or the legacy her two famous parents had left her. And time was running out because sooner than she'd like, she had to return to Hollywood to begin filming her next movie. The contract had been inked months ago and to back out at this late date would tarnish her name in the industry, not to mention the penalties she'd be subjected to for failure to perform.

But most of all, she took pride in standing by her word. When she said she'd do something, she did it. So not only would she do the movie, but she would also get this screenplay written over the holiday break—before she went back and faced the public scandal of her life.

She wanted to find a place on the second floor to write—away from Jackson. But she was still worried about him. His injury was serious, and he was overdoing things. Try as she might to keep him in bed, he never stayed more than five minutes at a time.

There was a desk with a lamp in the corner of the great room and that was where Serena took a seat with her laptop. This was one of those five-minute periods where Jackson was in the bedroom with his foot up. Gizmo was lying on a padded bench next to the window, watching the snow blow around in between snoozes. Now was her chance to get some work done.

She opened her laptop and after she logged in, her script popped up on the screen. She quickly read over what she'd written last night before she went to sleep. It didn't sound too bad, but something was missing. She just couldn't put her finger on what it was. Perhaps if she kept going, it would come to her. She hoped.

Serena's fingers moved rapidly over the keyboard. This screenplay might not be a serious drama, but it wasn't slapstick comedy, either. It was filled with heart. For now, writing about a warm family with a central love story and a happily-ever-after made her happy. It was about a loving but complicated family that she wished she'd been a part of. In the future, she intended to work on screenplays with more serious scenarios.

She paused and smiled. Perhaps writing an award-worthy screenplay wasn't as important as writing the story of her heart. Who knew, maybe it'd be prize-worthy after all. It might be a little zealous, but wasn't that what dreams were meant for?

For now, she'd chosen a shopaholic heroine and her large, boisterous family. Her ex-boyfriend needed a wife to keep his wealthy grandmother from writing him out of her will and leaving it all to her favorite pet charity. The hero was all about getting the money and pretending to be what his grandmother wanted him to be that he missed the point that money couldn't make you happy. And the heroine had to learn that a bigger wardrobe and a larger apartment wouldn't change who she was and that she hasdto accept herself, blemishes and all.

The more Serena typed, the more she worried whether she was going in the right direction with the plotline. Still, she kept pushing forward one word at a time—one sentence after the next—

Knock. Knock.

She jumped. She'd been so involved in her script that she hadn't heard anyone approach the door. Gizmo must have been sound asleep, too, because it wasn't until the knock that he starting barking as he scrambled to the door.

Serena jumped to her feet. "Gizmo, quiet."

The pup paused to look at her as though to ask why in the world he would want to be quiet when there was obviously an intruder on the premises. Immediately he went to his growl-bark, growl-bark stance.

"Who is it?" Jackson asked from behind her.

"I'm just about to find out—if I can get Gizmo to settle down." She bent down and picked up the dog.

The pup gave her a wide-eyed stare but at least he quieted down. With him securely in one arm, she opened the door. She couldn't help but wonder if it was another stranded person. "Can I help you?"

It was a man in a red snowsuit with a white cross on the left side. "I stopped to make sure you are okay." He spoke English with a heavy German accent.

"We are." She noticed how Jackson limped over to stand behind her. "Are you with the leasing company?"

"I'm not. I'm with the emergency crew working on clearing the avalanche, but they let us know that an American woman was staying here, and that you are by yourself, which I see you're not."

Jackson cleared his throat. "They must have cleared the road."

Serena peered past the man, looking for his vehicle in the freshly shoveled driveway. There was no vehicle. Maybe he left it on the road, but she didn't see it there, either. Surely the man didn't walk here. This cabin was in the middle of nowhere and this wasn't the weather for walking.

The man lifted his sunglasses and rested them on the top of his head. "Actually, I'm getting around on my snowmobile."

As the wind kicked up, Serena said, "Why don't you come inside?"

They moved back and let the man in the door. The man stepped forward just enough to close the door against the cold air. He was shorter than Jackson and had a much more stocky build. His face was tan, as though he spent a lot of time outside, and his eyes were kind.

The man cleared his throat. "The avalanche was bad. It has a stretch of road shut down until we can get equipment in to clear it." The man glanced around. "I see they got the power fixed."

"Not yet," Serena said. "It's a generator."

The man nodded in understanding. "They are hoping to get the power restored to this area sometime today."

Since this man seemed quite knowledgeable about their situation, she asked, "Do you know how long it will be until the road is open?"

He shook his head. "I have no idea."

"The thing is, Mr. Bennett here was in a car accident and I need to get him to the doctor—"

"I'm fine," Jackson interjected.

A concerned look came over the emergency worker's face as he turned to Jackson. His gaze scanned him. "I'm trained in first aid. Why don't you sit down on the couch and let me look at you. We can call in an emergency helicopter if we need to. It'll be tricky under these conditions but not impossible."

Jackson frowned. "I told you I'm fine."

"And I would like to see this for myself." The emergency worker gave him a pointed look.

They continued to stare at each other in that stubborn male fashion. It was really quite ridiculous. Why did Jackson have to be so stubborn?

Serena stepped forward. "Jackson." When he didn't look at her, she tried again. "Jackson, let him look at you. I'd feel much better if he did."

At last, Jackson turned to her. "I told you not to worry."

It was on the tip of her tongue to tell him that she did worry about him, but she stopped herself just in time. What in the world had gotten into her? She barely even knew this man. He might be amazingly handsome and she might be able to listen to his rich, deep voice for hours on end, but she had sworn off men. So she would be fine admiring Mr. Jackson Bennett via her television because that was as close as she planned to get to him once they could get away from this cabin.

Serena could feel both men staring at her. Heat swirled in her chest, but she refused to let that stop her from being honest—or at least partially honest. "I'd feel a lot better if someone who knew something about medicine would have a look at you. That was a bad accident. You have a lot of bruising. And your ankle doesn't look good."

Jackson sighed. "All right. If it's really that important to you."

"It is."

Jackson limped toward the couch.

"I'll be right back," the emergency worker said. "I have medical supplies on my snowmobile."

Serena followed Jackson. He sat on the couch and put his injured leg up on the coffee table. She knelt down on the floor and set Gizmo next to her. Finally, the pup had settled down. She didn't know what had gotten into him. He was usually friendlier. After all, he'd taken to Jackson.

She reached for the makeshift bandage.

"What are you doing?" Jackson asked.

"Taking off the bandage so he can have a look at you."

"I can do it."

She'd already started undoing the knot that she'd made to hold everything in place. "Just relax." She continued to struggle with the bandage. "I almost have it."

"It might be easier if you use scissors."

She didn't respond. The truth was that he was right, but when she was around him, her thoughts became jumbled. And when she touched him, her heart raced. What was it about this man that had her reacting like she was once again a schoolgirl with a crush on Jeremy Jones, the school's up-and-coming rock band singer?

She'd never felt this rush of emotions when she had been with Shawn. Sure, she'd enjoyed their time together, but she hadn't felt like it was anything special. Maybe she should have realized it was a sign that things weren't right. But she'd never been in love before, so she didn't know how it should feel. And now she never would know, because she was avoiding men—unless they unexpectedly crashed into her life.

Finally, the knot gave way. She made quick work of undoing the bandage. As much as she'd wished his ankle had healed quickly, it remained a kaleidoscope of colors from purplish black to red and some pink. What a mess.

Just then the door opened and Gizmo once more went into guard dog mode. Serena followed him to the doorway, where he had the emergency worker pinned to the door. Serena rushed over to pick up Gizmo.

The man had his hands full of medical supplies. If she were to go by looks, it appeared this man knew what he was doing. And that would be good for all of them because she was so far removed from a nurse that it wasn't even funny.

"I'm sorry," she said. "He's not normally like

this." When Gizmo started barking again, she said firmly, "Gizmo, stop." The dog didn't even bother to look at her as he kept a close eye on the stranger. "I'll just go put him in the bedroom."

Fifteen minutes later, Jackson had been all checked out. The emergency worker said that he didn't believe Jackson's injuries were life-threatening, but he was certainly banged up. If Jackson wanted to be evacuated, he'd call in a chopper. Jackson adamantly declined, saying that with the avalanche there were others in more need than him. And Serena promised to keep a close eye on him.

With Jackson in a proper bandage, the emergency worker packed up his stuff and walked away. Just as he opened the door, the light bulbs brightened, signaling that the electricity had been restored.

"Thank goodness," Serena said. "Things are starting to look up."

"I'll be back to check on you tomorrow." And with that the man left.

Serena closed the door. "Sounds like I better let Gizmo out before he scratches the door. I don't know what's up with him."

"He's just protective of you."

"Then how do you explain him taking to you?"

"Oh, that's easy, I bribed him." An easy smile pulled at Jackson's lips.

Serena's stomach dipped. Okay, it was official, he was much cuter in person than he was on television. And if she didn't get him out of here soon, he might worm his way past her defenses. But would that be so bad?

After all, they were on two different coasts. Surely with all those states between them and their busy schedules, they'd never lay eyes on each other again.

She shook her head. Obviously she wasn't used to the solitude. Everything would be fine. She would stick to her resolution of no men. Soon the plows would open up the road and Jackson would be on his way out of here.

"What?" Jackson's eyes filled with confusion.

"Hmm..."

"You shook your head. Why?"

"Nothing." She hunted for a legitimate answer to his question. "I should have figured that you would resort to bribing."

"It wasn't my idea." Jackson said it as though it were the undeniable truth. "Gizmo stole my bread last night and well, I didn't rat him out and we've been friends since."

"And it only cost you a slice of bread?"

Jackson smiled and her stomach once again

did that funny dipping thing. "Yeah, I guess it was worth sacrificing part of my dinner."

"And that would explain why he wasn't very interested in his." She planted her hands on her hips. "I don't want him eating human food so if you could refrain from feeding him in the future, I would appreciate it."

"I'll try, but no promises." When she arched a brow, he added, "Hey, he's sneaky."

"Uh-huh." Was it possible that this journalist was truly a big softy at heart?

The thought stuck with her as she went to turn off the generator. She really wanted to dislike Jackson. It would make this arrangement so much easier, but the more time she spent with him, the more she liked him.

CHAPTER EIGHT

THE DAY SLIPPED by very slowly.

Jackson didn't know what to do with himself. He wasn't good at sitting still and yet his ankle, though most likely not broken, was still severely bruised and swollen.

He picked up his cell phone from the coffee table. He put in his passcode only to find that there was still no signal. So much for them getting the cell tower fixed today...or whatever was causing the disruption in service. He knew he shouldn't complain. With the avalanche, everyone had much larger concerns.

He tossed the phone back on the coffee table and sighed.

Mae glanced up from her laptop. "Do you need something?"

"Yes. I mean, no."

"So which is it?"

He limped over to her desk. "I'm just bored, is all. I'm not used to having time on my hands. Usually I don't have enough hours in the day to get things done. Today I don't have enough things to do."

"I understand. My life is usually very hectic. That's one thing I love about being here. No one can bother me and I can make my own schedule."

"So what has you so busy on the computer for hours on end?"

"This, oh, well…it's nothing."

Was it his imagination or did her cheeks take on a shade of pink? His curiosity grew. She closed the laptop and stood. He couldn't take his eyes off her as she stretched.

"You don't strike me as a shy woman. So what has you blushing when I asked about what you were working on?"

Her fine brows drew together. "And you are not on the job. I'm not one of your stories. You don't have to keep pushing until you get all of the answers."

Realizing that he'd overstepped, he held up both hands. "Sorry. I guess this sitting around is really starting to get to me. I think I've read every magazine on the coffee table at least twice."

"Then I can put you to work." Her eyes lit up as though she'd come up with the perfect answer.

He was intrigued. He'd love to spend some productive time with Mae. Perhaps his abundance of enthusiasm should bother him, but he chose to ignore the telling sign. "What do you have in mind?"

"I'll be right back." She took off upstairs.

Gizmo got up from where he'd been napping on the couch. When he yawned, he let out a little squeak. Jackson found himself smiling. Gizmo walked over to him. Jackson petted him and scratched behind his ears.

"You're not so bad. In fact, you're kind of cute."

"Arff!"

Jackson couldn't help but laugh. "You know, if I didn't know better, I'd say you knew what I was saying."

"Arff! Arff!"

"Sounds like you two are having quite a conversation," Mae said as she descended the stairs with her hands full of bags.

"And what is all of that?" He had a feeling he didn't want to know, but the reporter in him needed the answer.

"This is what we're going to do this evening. And if you do a good job, I'll let you roast some marshmallows over the fire tonight."

He couldn't help but laugh again. He tried to remember the last time he'd laughed this much and failed. Was there such a time?

He didn't think so, as June had been more reserved. She was quiet in public. She would say that it was the way she was raised, but he knew the truth—she was painfully shy. Still, she hadn't let it stop her as a fashion model. Each day she did what was expected of her. And although it took a lot out of her to get in front of the cameras, she'd pasted on a smile and never missed a photo shoot.

But there had been times when she'd let her hair down and unwind when they were in bed. Then she'd been all his. And there had been nothing shy about her then. He could make her laugh, moan and make all sorts of unladylike sounds—

Jackson squelched the memories. He wanted to be present in this moment. He took in Mae's smile. It lit up her face and made her eyes sparkle, but it was more than that. How did he say it? It was like when she smiled the world was brighter. It filled him with a warmth, and he never wanted to let that feeling go. It healed the cracks in his broken heart, making him feel whole again.

"Can you make your way over here?" she asked as she set the bags down in front of the Christmas tree.

And then he put it all together. He shook his head. "I don't do Christmas trees."

Her eyes widened. "You don't celebrate Christmas?"

"No. Not that. I celebrate it—or I used to.

But I never did the decorating." The truth was, with busy work schedules that often conflicted, neither he nor June were home long enough to worry about it. Instead, June would hire professionals to come in and decorate their tree. It was always different each year. Different color. Different theme.

Mae stood there with a puzzled look on her face. "Why wouldn't you decorate your tree? Doesn't it look rather sad and pathetic without ornaments?"

"It had ornaments. I just didn't put them on."

"Why not?"

"There wasn't enough time." That seemed to be the theme of his life. There were so many things that had been skipped over or missed because there wasn't enough time. And now time had run out for him and June.

"You have to make time for the important things in life. My father used to always put off things and then he died." There was a slight pause, but before Jackson could say a word, she continued. "I don't want to miss the good things in life because I'm too busy. Life is too short."

It was as though she understood exactly what he'd been through, but that was impossible. He kept his private life private. "I'm glad you're taking advantage of life. You're right, it is too short."

She reached into the bag and pulled out a box of ornaments. She proceeded to attach a hook and hang it on the tree. "See. Nothing to it. Come on. Decorate it with me. I already strung the lights the other night."

But it was more than the fact that he didn't have experience at trimming a Christmas tree— everything about the season would remind him of June. It would be a painful reminder of all that he'd lost. Christmastime was the time of year June loved the most. It was when she was at her best—when they had been at their best.

"Jackson?" Mae's voice jerked him from his thoughts.

He shook his head. "I don't think this is a good idea."

"Sure, it is. After all, it's almost Christmas."

"But this is your tree, not mine." He knew it was a lame excuse, but he just couldn't bring himself to admit the truth—he felt guilty celebrating without June.

"For as long as you're here with me, it's our tree. Yours, mine and Gizmo's." At that point, the dog's ears perked up. Mae turned to her pup and said, "Isn't that right, boy?"

As if on cue, Gizmo barked. Spontaneous laughter erupted in Jackson. These two seemed determined to cheer him up. And it was working.

He normally wasn't that easily amused, but

being around Mae and her dog was bringing out a whole new side in him. And he honestly didn't know what to make of it—what to make of the way Mae made him feel.

This isn't a good idea.
It'll be fine.

The conflicting thoughts piled one on top of the other. But it came down to the fact that Serena felt sorry for Jackson. How could a man who appeared to have everything miss out on the spirit of Christmas?

To her, Christmastime was going beyond your normal comfort zone in order to lend others a helping hand. She tried to do it year-round, but filming schedules usually upended her best efforts to visit the soup kitchen during the rest of the year.

She'd been doing it for years now. At first, she'd done it in defiance of her father, who'd said that no Winston should be pandering to others. How she was related to that man was beyond her. They disagreed about most everything. When she was young, she used to wonder if they'd mixed up the babies in the hospital nursery. She'd even said it once to her father— he hadn't taken it well, at all.

But the more time she spent at the soup kitchen, the more she liked the people there.

She soon learned that her attendance wasn't so much about what she could give them but rather what they gave her. They reminded her that there was so much more to life than money and contracts. Because in the end, it was about love and kindness.

Of course, none of those people knew her true identity, either. She'd always wear a wig and dress in baggy T-shirts and faded jeans that she'd picked up at a secondhand store. She'd quickly learned just how comfortable those casual clothes could be—

"And what are you thinking about?" Jackson asked as he placed a hook on a glass ornament.

What would it hurt to share her thoughts? After all, they were living here together for the foreseeable future. It wasn't like she was going to open up and spill her whole life story.

"I was thinking about what I would be doing now if I were at home."

"Let me guess, shopping at the mall. Your arms would be full of shopping bags with gifts for your family."

She shook her head. "Not even close."

He blinked as though shocked by her denial. "Hmm…let's see. You'd be on holiday on a cruise ship."

"Although I like the way you think, that's not it."

He shrugged. "Okay. I give up. What would you be doing?"

"Working in a soup kitchen."

He didn't say anything, but the shock was quite vivid in his eyes. And he wouldn't stop staring. He made her want to squirm, but she held her ground.

"Why are you looking like I joined the circus?"

He visibly swallowed. "I'm sorry. I think what you do is great. It's just that I'm not used to people around me being so giving with their time. Everything in my world is rush-rush."

Surely he couldn't be that impressed. She'd watched his show regularly and knew that he attended fund-raisers. "And if you were in New York, what would you be doing?"

He shrugged. "Not much."

"But it's the holidays. Come on. Maybe you'd be attending some prestigious event."

He shook his head. She glanced into his eyes and noticed how the light in them had dimmed. And then it dawned on her that the look in his eyes was one of pain and loss. His wife had died a while back. And now that she thought about it, she hadn't glimpsed any photos of him at the various gala events since his wife had passed away.

So he knew what it was like to lose someone close—just like she'd lost her father. Even though her parental relationship had been complicated, it didn't mean that she hadn't loved him.

"My...my wife," Jackson said, drawing Serena from her thoughts, "she was always busy with one charity group or another. I don't attend the fund-raising events now—not without her."

The way his voice cracked with emotion didn't get past Serena. She recalled how he and his wife had appeared inseparable. It seemed like every Monday morning there were photos of them on *Hello America*. Serena recalled how they always looked so happy—so in love. It was obvious that he was still in love with her.

Serena's gaze immediately sought out his left hand. No ring. And then realizing what she was doing, she glanced away. There may no longer be a physical link to his wife, but in his heart, he would always love her. The proof was in the pain reflected in his eyes and the catch in his voice when he spoke of her.

"I'm sorry for your loss." And now she understood why he wasn't anxious to decorate the Christmas tree. It probably reminded him of his wife and their holidays together. "If you don't want to help me, that's okay. I'm sure celebrating Christmas alone isn't easy."

He continued putting hooks on the ornaments. "I lost her a couple of years ago." He paused as though that was all he was going to say. "At first, after she died, I didn't know how I was going to go on. We did everything together. She even traveled with me when I did travel segments for the morning show."

"Did you two make it to Austria? Is that why you're here?"

He shook his head. "She didn't like snow. I had the option of picking the places for the Christmas segment. And I wanted something different—a place without memories."

Serena was surprised that he was opening up to her. It made her feel guilty for keeping so much of herself a secret. But a part of her liked having him treat her like a normal human being and not like a superstar or a part of Hollywood royalty.

Her parents had had the most notorious, glamorous love story on-and off-screen. There was even a movie about their stormy, passionate relationship. Serena had never watched it and never planned to. She'd been there for the real thing and that had been enough for her. Real life was never like the lives portrayed on the big screen. In fact, in her case, reality was as far from glamorous as you could get.

Serena was lost in the past when Jackson spoke.

"What about you? Why aren't you with your family?"

This was her moment to solidify whatever this was growing between them. Dare she call it a friendship? She glanced at him. At that moment, he looked up and their gaze caught and held. Her heart beat wildly. Friendship wasn't exactly the only thing she was feeling where he was concerned.

No other man had ever made her feel this way. Sure there were gorgeous on-screen heroes. But she never let herself get caught in those romances. Growing up in a Hollywood family, she knew that love was fleeting at best. And then she'd met Shawn. It'd been after her father's death and perhaps her defenses had been down. Whatever the reason, she'd let him into her life. And what a mistake that had been.

But she wasn't going to repeat that mistake by making another one with a world-renowned television journalist. With all her effort, she glanced away. She turned to climb the ladder to place the ornament high up on the tree.

"Aren't you going to share?" he asked.

She did owe him an answer. It wasn't fair to expect him to open up when she wasn't prepared to do the same. "My father died last year. I don't have a reason to be home."

"I'm sorry." There was a pause as though he

was considering what to say next. "What about your mother?"

"She's off on a Caribbean cruise with her latest boyfriend." She didn't bother to add that the aforementioned boyfriend was Serena's age. "My mother was never very maternal or traditional."

Jackson didn't say anything. He probably didn't know what to say because he'd had the idyllic childhood and the picture-perfect family. She was happy for him, but sad for herself. Some would say that it made her a stronger person, but she just thought it made her more cynical about life.

Jackson moved to the ladder to hand her another ornament. "Mae, I'm sorry."

She turned to tell him that he didn't have to be sorry. But before she could tell him, she dropped the Christmas ball. It fell to the floor and Gizmo let out an excited bark. He'd been waiting all this time for something to play with.

"No, Gizmo."

But it was too late. The dog chased the ball under the ladder. She moved too quickly. She'd never know if it was her sudden shift in weight or Gizmo running into the ladder, but the old wooden ladder swayed. Serena reached out, but there was nothing to grab onto. The ladder tilted to one side.

Serena started to fall. A shriek tore from her lungs.

And then her body crashed into Jackson's.

His strong arms wrapped around her. "It's okay. I've got you."

"Gizmo?"

"Is fine."

She turned her head to thank Jackson and that was when she realized just how close they were. She breathed in his scent—a mix of soap and pure masculinity. It was quite a heady combo.

For a moment, neither spoke. They didn't move as they stared deep into each other's eyes. It was just as well that he didn't say a word, because she'd have never heard him over the pounding of her heart. In fact, it was so loud that it drowned out any common sense.

She was in the arms of Jackson Bennett—her morning eye candy. He was the man that she had had a secret crush on for years now. How was it possible that it took them both traveling to Europe for their paths to cross? When people said that life was stranger than fiction, they were right.

And then his gaze dipped down to her lips. He was going to kiss her. The breath caught in her throat. She'd always wondered what it would be like to be kissed by him. And this was her one and only chance to answer that question.

With the Christmas lights twinkling in the background, Serena's eyes drifted closed. Letting go completely of the ramifications of her actions and just giving in to what she wanted, she leaned forward. His lips pressed to hers.

The kiss was slow and tender. After being unceremoniously groped in the past by eager suitors, this cautious approach caught her off guard. As the kiss progressed, she realized that Jackson was unlike any of the other men in her past.

She wondered what it would be like to have a real relationship with a mature, self-assured man like Jackson. While she could never picture herself long term with Shawn, she could envision a life with Jackson—marriage, kids, the whole nine yards!

The image was so real—so vivid that it startled her.

She pulled back. Her eyes fluttered open. As soon as his gaze met hers, heat rushed to her face. She felt exposed and vulnerable.

She knew that there was no way he could read her thoughts, but that didn't ease her discomfort. Of all the men to imagine a future with, Jackson wasn't the right one. He still loved his late wife.

Jackson didn't say a word as he lowered her legs to the floor. He went to straighten the ladder before he retrieved the Christmas ornament from Gizmo. And all that time, Serena stood there trying to make sense of what had just happened.

That kiss had been like a window into the future. But how was that possible? She immediately dismissed the ludicrous thought.

But she was left with one question. Now that they'd kissed, how did they go back to that easy, friendly coexistence? Because every time her gaze strayed to him, she'd be fantasizing about what would have happened if she hadn't pulled away.

CHAPTER NINE

THE NEXT MORNING, Jackson made his way to the kitchen. He yawned. He'd been restless most of the night. All the while, he'd been plagued by memories of the kiss. It had been an amazing kiss. The kind of kiss that could make a man forget his pledge of solitude—forget the risk he'd be taking with his heart if he were to let someone get close.

Even knowing the risks, there was a part of him that wished it hadn't ended. Chemistry like that didn't happen every day. In fact, he'd be willing to bet that it only happened once in a lifetime.

His thoughts had circled around all night, from how much he wanted to seek out Mae and pull her close to continue that kiss to wondering why he'd let his resolve weaken. What had he been thinking to kiss Mae? And what did that say about his devotion to June?

He still loved June. He always would. That acknowledgment only compounded his guilt.

And now what must Mae be thinking? She hadn't seemed interested in him. In fact, in the beginning he wasn't even certain that she was going to let him seek shelter from the storm in her cabin. But had that kiss complicated their relationship?

He paused at the kitchen doorway, not sure what to say to her. Perhaps it was best to act as though the kiss had never happened. With that thought, he pushed open the door.

An array of cereal boxes sat on the table next to an empty bowl and fresh orange slices. It appeared Mae had been up early that morning. He wondered if she'd had problems sleeping, too. He scanned the kitchen but didn't find any sign of her.

Gizmo came wandering into the kitchen.

"Hey, little guy, where's your momma?"

For once, the pup didn't say anything. Instead, Gizmo yawned. It appeared no one in the cabin had slept well. Maybe it was just from being cooped up for so long. But he knew that wasn't the case. It was the kiss…

Every time he'd closed his eyes, Mae's image had been there. It wasn't right. He shouldn't have done it. He shouldn't have gotten caught up in the moment.

He knew that June was gone and was never coming back, but he'd promised to love her forever. He also recalled how June had made him promise to move on with his life—to love again. The painful memories came flooding back.

June had been so unwell and yet her last thought had been of him. He hadn't kept his promise—at least not until now. Not that he was going to pursue Mae. He just couldn't move on as though June had never been a huge part of his life. How could he put his heart on the line again?

The grief of losing June had cost him dearly. The thought of being so vulnerable again had him withdrawing from friends and social settings. Until Mae…

She made him remember how things used to be—think of how things could be if he'd let himself go. She made him feel alive again. He shook his head to clear his thoughts, but it didn't work. Mae was still there in the front of his mind.

With a sigh, he sat down at the table and filled the bowl with corn flakes. He didn't really have an appetite, but his stomach growled in protest. Perhaps some food would help his attitude.

He glanced down to find Gizmo had wandered off, leaving Jackson alone with his thoughts. The cabin was quiet. As he stared out the window, he was pleased to find the sun was out. Today would be the day when he was able to get on with his life. He knew the thought of leaving here should bring him a sense of relief but it didn't.

The truth was, he'd really enjoyed the time he'd spent with Mae. She had a way about her that put him at ease. Maybe it was because they'd each shared a recent loss or the fact that neither had a loving, devoted mother. Whatever you wanted to say, they shared a special connection. One he wouldn't soon forget.

But Christmas was only a week away and if he didn't get this last segment shot, it'd be too late to air. The slot would get filled and everyone would move on.

If only he could put a special spin on this segment, something more than Christmas in a quaint village in Austria. He knew what they'd already planned would pull on the viewers' nostalgic heartstrings, but his thoughts needed to be on the head honchos in the front office. He only had until the first of the year to prove that he was the man for the evening news slot.

Jackson heard the kitchen door creak open. He turned expecting to find Mae, but instead it was once again Gizmo. He strolled back into the kitchen with something in his mouth. Jackson smiled and shook his head. That dog was forever stealing things. He wondered if Mae would find everything the dog had stolen before she left here. Well, he could help her out this time.

He got up and approached Gizmo. "Hey, boy, what do you have there?"

The dog tried to get around him, but Jackson blocked him. That definitely wasn't a dog toy in his mouth, and this time it wasn't a pink lacy bra, either. The memory of that piece of lingerie combined with the kiss last night heated his veins—

No. Don't go there. It was a onetime thing. Let it go.

He knelt down to pet the dog. Luckily his ankle was starting to feel a bit better with the aid of over-the-counter painkillers. Still, he kept his weight on his good leg.

His fingers wrapped around what appeared to be Mae's wallet. "Give it to me."

Gizmo clenched tighter and started to pull back. He gave a little growl, all the while wagging his tail. Gizmo's head shook back and forth as he tried to work the wallet away from Jackson.

"You're a strong little guy, aren't you?"

Gizmo let out another little growl as his tail continued to swish back and forth.

Well, this was one game of tug-of-war Jackson didn't want to lose.

"Let go." No such luck. "Gizmo! Stop."

Suddenly, Gizmo let go.

Not prepared for the dog's sudden release,

Jackson fell backward. He lost his grip on the wallet as he tried to catch himself. He landed squarely on his backside.

Gizmo didn't tarry. He turned to make his escape. Jackson sat on the floor and watched as the dog pushed the swinging door open with his nose.

Jackson couldn't help but smile and shake his head. He wondered if this was what it was like having small children. He would never know since he and June were never blessed with any. It was yet another thing that they'd put off too long—another dream that would never be fulfilled.

He went to pick up Mae's wallet when he realized that it had come open and some of the cards had scattered across the tile floor. He picked them up and started putting them in the wallet when he noticed the name on them: Serena Winston.

He immediately recognized the name. How could he not? Serena Winston came from a legendary family. He'd tried repeatedly to interview her, but for one reason or another, it had never worked out.

This had to be some sort of mix-up. The Serena Winston on these cards couldn't be the famous actress. But if that was the case, why did Mae have them? He held the California driver's license closer. He studied the similarities. If Mae were to be a blonde and add makeup—

His mouth gaped.

It was her. The driver's license read: *Serena M. Winston.*

Serena Mae Winston?

Jackson sat there stunned. He'd thought that they'd formed a friendship. He'd trusted her with intimate details of his life, but she hadn't even been honest about her name—at least not her whole name.

Everything started to fall in place, such as her ability to lease this luxury cabin for herself and her dog. She'd been hiding in plain sight with her strawberry blonde hair and lack of makeup. He'd never seen any photos of Serena Winston with reddish hair. She was known far and wide for her honey-blond strands. And it explained what had happened to her—how she was able to drop off the radar.

His thoughts circled back to how he'd believed that they were beginning to trust each other. Then there was that kiss—the kiss he hadn't been able to forget no matter how hard he tried. Well, he no longer had to worry about it. Obviously, it had been all one-sided. All the time, she'd been playing him for a fool.

Anger warmed his veins. He didn't like to be lied to. His gut knotted at the thought of her laughing behind his back. He wished this was some sort of dream because he'd liked Mae—a woman who didn't even exist. Why couldn't just one thing in his life go his way?

He stuffed her cards back in the wallet. He got to his feet. With the breakfast dishes and food long forgotten, he headed out of the kitchen to find his hostess. The jig was up and he intended to tell her.

He'd just reached the living room when his cell phone rang. At last, the cell tower had been fixed. But it couldn't have been worse timing. The only person he wanted to speak to was Mae—erm, Serena. But he didn't see her at the desk working on her laptop. Nor was she on the couch. He could only guess that she was upstairs. And he wasn't sure his ankle was up for that particular challenge.

The buzzing of his phone would not stop. He withdrew it from his pants pocket and checked the caller ID. It was his agent. And it wasn't the first time Fred had called. There was a long list of missed calls. He must be worried about Jackson disappearing, especially at such a pivotal time in his career.

Jackson's gaze returned to the grand stairs leading to the second floor. The phone vibrated in his hand. He sighed and accepted the call.

"Jackson, thank goodness. What happened to you?"

"I was involved in a car accident."

"Accident? Are you hurt? Did you injure your face?"

Leave it to Fred to get to the heart of his concern—Jackson's marketability. "My face is fine."

"You're sure?"

"Yes."

"Well, where are you? The crew has been looking for you. They aren't sure what to do."

"I'm snowed in." He headed for Mae...erm... Serena's desk in the great room to drop off the wallet. "And you'll never believe who rescued me..."

CHAPTER TEN

THE KISS MEANT NOTHING.

Nothing at all.

That was what Serena had been telling herself ever since last night, when she'd fallen into Jackson's more-than-capable arms. What had she been thinking to kiss the enemy?

Who was she kidding? Jackson wasn't the enemy, even if he was part of the news media. Maybe at first she hadn't trusted him—with her background, who could blame her? But during the time they'd spent together, she'd learned that there was so much more to him than his dashing looks and his day job.

He was a man who'd loved and lost. He was kind and generous. He went out of his way for others, even when he'd rather be doing anything else. And he had a sense of humor. The memory of his deep laugh still sent goose bumps down her arms. That was a sound she could listen to for the rest of her life—

Whoa! Slow down.

She knew that this moment of playing house would end soon—just as soon as the avalanche was cleared and they were able to plow the roads. Then they would return to reality, but for now, they lived within their own little world with their own rules and she intended to enjoy it as long as it lasted.

And if that should include some more kisses?

Well, she wouldn't complain. An impish smile pulled at her lips.

She'd been kissed by a lot of leading men, but none of them could come close to Jackson. That man was made for kissing. Just the memory of his lips pressed to hers had her sighing. It hadn't lasted long enough, not even close.

And now, instead of kissing that handsome man, she was doing his laundry. Something wasn't right about that. But she was proud of herself for being able to take care of herself. Neither of her parents knew how to work a washing machine much less the dryer. They'd always been dependent on domestic help.

Serena learned early on that if she wanted true privacy, she had to be self-sufficient. And to be honest, she was never quite comfortable with people waiting on her. Maybe it was the time she'd spent serving food at the soup kitchen—seeing people who barely made it day to day—that had opened her eyes to the extravagances that her parents took for granted.

Whatever it was, she'd learned to do everything for herself except cooking. She had yet to master it. But she could clean the bathroom and iron her clothes.

It was only recently when her filming schedule became so out of control that she'd taken on a housekeeper. It was only supposed to be temporary, but Mrs. Martinez was so sweet and in desperate need of work that Serena kept her on.

Sometimes Serena missed doing the laundry. She found it relaxing. But doing Jackson's laundry had extra benefits, like the lingering hint of his cologne on his laundered shirts. She stood in the master suite next to the closet sniffing his shirt. If he were to walk in now and catch her, she would die of mortification. She was acting like some teenager—

There were footsteps followed by Jackson's voice. Was he talking to Gizmo? But she didn't have time to contemplate the answer as she was still clenching his shirt.

Not about to be caught acting like a lovesick puppy, she stepped into the closet and slid the door shut. She had to hunch over in order to fit. Why couldn't this closet be a walk-in? But no, it had to be long and skinny. And there was a hanger digging into her shoulder blade. She started to move when the metal hangers jingled together. She froze in place.

What was she doing in here?

Plain and simple, she'd panicked.

What was it about Jackson's presence that short-circuited her thought process? She never had this problem with any other man in her life. Jackson was unique.

She was about to open the door and step out when she heard her name mentioned. The breath caught in her throat as she strained to catch what he was saying about her.

"I'm serious. Serena Winston saved my life."

There was a pause. He must be talking on the phone. That meant the cell service and internet were back online. She didn't know if that was a blessing or a curse. She supposed she would soon find out.

"Don't you dare say a word. I told you that as my friend, not my agent." A pause ensued. "Because I told you not to. Just leave it be."

Serena smiled. Jackson was protecting her privacy. He was a bona fide hero in her book.

"Hey, Gizmo." Pause. "No. I was talking to the dog."

Oh, no. If Gizmo realized she was in the closet, he would put up a fuss. No sooner had the thought passed through her mind than there was the sound of pawing at the door. Serena didn't move. She didn't so much as take a breath. She just prayed that Gizmo would get bored and move on.

"Arff! Arff!"

"Are you serious? She's all over the headlines?" Another pause. "I don't need to check it out." Pause. "Yes. I know this scoop could make a difference in my career, but it's not worth it to me."

Serena smiled broadly and pumped her fist, banging her hand into more hangers. *Jingle. Jingle.* She reached up, silencing the hangers. The last thing she needed was for him to catch her lurking in his closet. She didn't even want to imagine what she must look like. This was easily the most embarrassing moment of her life—and if Jackson caught her, it would be even worse.

"Arff! Arff!"
Scratch. Scratch. Scratch.

"Stop… No, not you. I was talking to the dog. Listen, I've got to go take the dog out." Pause. "I don't know." Pause. "As soon as they plow open the roads."

Jackson's footsteps could be heard approaching the closet. "There's nothing in there, boy. Come on. I'll take you out."

Jackson's footsteps faded away.

Serena cautiously exhaled a pent-up breath.

She opened the closet door a crack to make sure the coast was clear. It was. She quickly exited and stretched. Her muscles did not like being hunched over for so long.

Not wasting too much time, she hung up the shirt, closed the closet and exited Jackson's bedroom. She glanced toward the front porch, where she saw him through the window. His ankle must be feeling a lot better if he could put on a boot and go out in the snow. That was good, right?

For some reason, the thought of Jackson being mobile didn't make her happy. Soon he'd be leaving her. And now that she knew she could trust him, she wanted him to stay.

The only question she had was whether he'd known who she was all along. If not, what had tipped him off?

She carried the now-empty laundry basket back to the laundry room just off the kitchen. As she placed it on the floor next to the dryer for another load, she realized that this place, even though it was quite large, was very homey. She'd never felt relaxed at her home in Hollywood.

And then she realized that perhaps it wasn't the structure around her but rather the people in it. Gizmo was new to her life and they'd immediately bonded. And now there was Jackson. She felt guilty for not trusting him sooner. Perhaps it wasn't too late to make it up to him.

She returned to the great room and was about to sit down at her laptop when she noticed her wallet sitting on the corner of her desk. How in the world had it gotten here? And then she noticed the distinct bite marks in the black leather. Gizmo. He was the one who'd given her away. *That dog.*

Just then the front door swung open. Gizmo raced into the room as though he were being chased. He stopped and shook himself off. Serena couldn't help but smile. This dog did not like snow.

"What's so amusing?" Jackson asked.

"Gizmo. He doesn't like the snow. At all."

"Give him time. It might grow on him."

Somehow she didn't think that would be the case. She glanced down at the wallet with bite marks. She supposed it was a little late to come clean considering Jackson knew the truth about her.

"I see you found the wallet," Jackson said. "I rescued it from Gizmo. I think he was planning to hide it."

"He is a bit of a thief. You better watch your stuff." How did she say this? Did she just apologize for keeping her true identity a secret? Would he understand?

Jackson said something.

"Hmm…" She'd been lost in her thoughts and hadn't caught all he'd said.

"I said your secret is safe with me."

It wasn't until her gaze met his dark, pointed stare that she knew she was in trouble. He was angry with her for keeping her identity from him. She didn't know what to say to undo things.

"I… I'm sorry," she said, but the words didn't seem to faze him. "I have a hard time trusting people."

"Do you know that there's a search on for you? It appears that your fiancé is heading it up. His face is all over the media sites begging for information about your whereabouts."

Her hands balled up at her sides. How dare Shawn act like he cared? It was all a show— just another way for him to benefit by linking himself to her.

"He's not my fiancé. We were never engaged— not even close."

Jackson's brows rose. "That's not what all of the tabloids are saying."

"Shawn would do anything for headlines, including feeding false information to the press. He doesn't like me, much less love me. I'm just a stepping-stone to his goals."

"Really?" Jackson sounded skeptical. "Why don't you tell people the truth about him?"

"Do you think they'd believe me? Anything I say will be twisted and blown up into an even bigger scandal. I just want it to all die down and go away. I want him to go away. I wish I'd never met him."

Jackson wore a puzzled expression. "And that's what you're doing here—hiding until the story dies?"

"In a manner of speaking." She didn't actually consider it hiding, but she wasn't going to argue semantics with him.

"From what my agent was telling me, the story is growing with every day you're gone." He raked his fingers through his hair. "It might be good to let someone know that you're alive and safe. Some tabloids have even surmised that you're dead. Others think you've been kidnapped."

"Seriously?" She shook her head and sat down at the desk. "Can't people mind their own business?"

"Is there anything I can do to help? Perhaps my agent could release a statement to put everyone at ease—"

"No. No statement."

"Okay. So what? You're just going to suddenly reappear one day?"

"Something like that."

She pulled up the tabloids on her laptop. The headlines were ridiculous. And below the headlines was a photo of a distraught Shawn. Her stomach churned. When was that guy going to get on with his life? She would give him this much, he was a great actor. Because if she didn't know that he was lying, she might have believed his show.

Unable to take any more of the lies and sensational journalism, she closed the laptop. "Listen, I'm sorry I wasn't up-front with you."

"I understand. At least now I do. When your driver's license fell on the floor, I wasn't very happy with you."

"I... I don't know what to say. I came here to be alone and then I thought—oh, I don't know what I thought. I should have told you, but I hadn't worked up the courage. It isn't easy for me to let people into my life."

He nodded as though he understood. "You've lived your entire life in front of the cameras. You don't know who you can trust. And with my occupation, I'm sure that didn't help things."

"You're right. It didn't. I was afraid that once you found out who I was, you would make me a headline on your morning news show."

When frown lines bracketed his eyes, she knew that she'd said too much. That was the thing about letting people get close. She wasn't sure how much to say and how much to hold back. At least when she was acting in front of the camera, she had printed lines to follow. She didn't have to figure out what to say, how much to say and when to say it.

That was another problem that kept her from seeking the spotlight. She was awkward in public. It would seem odd to most considering who her parents were and what she did for a living. But when she was in front of the cameras, she got to pretend that she was someone else—someone brave and ready to say their piece. However, Serena Mae Winston was a private person who struggled with the fame that her family lineage and job brought her.

Jackson cleared his throat. "I know we haven't known each other for long, but do I strike you as someone who would go behind someone's back to make a headline?"

"No." The look on his face said that he didn't believe her. "I mean it. I know we haven't known each other for long, but I... I trust you." He had no idea how hard that was for her to say.

His stance eased, as did the frown lines on his face. "Then maybe we should start over."

"Start over?"

He nodded. Then he approached her and held out his hand. "Hi. I'm Jackson Bennett. The face of *Hello America*."

She placed her hand in his and a warm sensation zinged up her arm. Her heart palpitated faster than normal. "Hi. I'm Serena Winston. I'm an actress who is trying to have a normal, quiet holiday."

"I'm happy to meet you, Serena—"

Just then there was a loud rumbling sound. It woke Gizmo from his nap on the couch. He started to bark as he ran to the door. Jackson and Serena followed.

"What do you think it is this time?" she asked.

"It's definitely not another avalanche. This is a much different sound." Jackson listened for a moment. "I think they are opening up the road."

"Really? We can get out of here?"

"You're that anxious to get rid of me?"

"I didn't say that, but we need to get you to the doctor to see if you did any serious damage to your leg."

"Do you really think I could walk on it if I had?"

"Is that what you call the motion you make?"

"Hey, I'm trying here."

"I know. I just worry that you're trying too hard and that you're going to do permanent damage to yourself."

As they were standing there next to the window talking, a red-and-black snowmobile cut across the front of the yard.

"Looks like that guy from the emergency crew is back to check on you," Serena said.

"I'm fine. You all need to quit worrying about me."

"If you were fine, you would walk normal."

Jackson grunted and limped over to the couch while Serena waited for their visitor to make it to the door.

CHAPTER ELEVEN

SHE WAS RIGHT.

But that knowledge didn't make Serena happy.

The official diagnosis was in. Jackson's ankle was fractured. Even the doctor was surprised that Jackson was able to get around as well as he had been. As it was, the doctor had set him up with a walking boot.

"We shouldn't be here," she said as they stood at the edge of the town square. "You should be at home resting your leg."

Jackson turned and stared into her eyes. "Have you ever been to a Christmas market?"

"Arff!"

Jackson smiled and gazed down at Gizmo. "I wasn't talking to you, boy." Jackson's gaze rose until it met Serena's again. "I was talking to you."

"Um, well, um…no. But I'm not exactly dressed for it."

His gaze skimmed over her white coat, red

scarf and faded jeans. "There's nothing wrong with what you're wearing."

She lifted a hand to her hair. "But I didn't do anything with my hair."

"You look cute with a ponytail. It suits you. You worry too much. You're beautiful just the way you are."

The way Jackson stared so deeply into her eyes made the rest of the world fade away. In that moment, it was as if just the two of them existed. He was staring at her like—like he wanted to kiss her.

Her gaze lowered, taking in his very tempting mouth. The thought of once again being held in his very capable arms and feeling his mouth pressed to hers was quite tempting. Was it possible that he was the first man to like her just the way she was?

Her father had always been disappointed in her. It didn't matter if it was her choice in movie roles or if it was the style of her haircut. She'd never gained his approval and then he'd died on her before anything could be resolved between them. One minute he was giving her a hard time about not aligning her romantic relationship with her career. And the next, he was lying on the floor, dead, from a massive heart attack. That was it. No time for "I love yous" or "goodbyes." It was just over—in a heartbeat.

Maybe that was why she let herself become involved with her leading man. Shawn was great-looking and he could say all the right things, but she soon learned that it was all a show. He was constantly acting, being whoever he needed to be to impress people—to get a leg up in the Hollywood world.

But Jackson didn't want anything from her. Not even an interview. He was the first man who'd ever been comfortable with who he was without having to put on a show for the public, which surprised her. After all, Jackson's career was about projecting a certain image for the public, but here he was with scruff on his jaw and his hair a little ruffled by the breeze and he wasn't the least bit worried about his appearance.

She liked being treated like a real person instead of a star. A smile lifted her lips. She liked Jackson. He was so different from the other men who had passed through her life.

"I don't know what's going through your mind," Jackson said, "but whatever it is, I approve. You should smile more often."

Just then Gizmo saw another dog. Being the friendly sort, he wanted to go visit. He started to run, but after walking in a circle, his leash was now wrapped around Jackson and herself. So when Gizmo ran out of length, the leash yanked them together.

Her hands pressed upon Jackson's very firm chest. She had to crane her neck to look into his eyes. It was then that his gaze moved to her lips. He lowered his head and immediately claimed her lips.

His kiss was gentle and sweet. It made her wish that they were back at the cabin where the kiss didn't have to end—where they could see where it would lead. Because she realized that their time together was almost at an end. Jackson would have to get back to the project that he'd flown to Austria to do, and she needed to add some serious word count to her screenplay if she wanted it ready for her agent when she returned to Hollywood. It would hopefully give the paparazzi something to talk about besides her scandalous love life.

"Arff! Arff!"

Their lips parted and they turned to Gizmo. He jumped up, placing his front paws on Jackson's good leg.

"I think someone wants to be picked up," Serena said.

"That might be easier if he hadn't wrapped us up in his leash."

"Maybe someone shouldn't have released so much of his leash."

Jackson's eyes widened. "You're blaming me for this?"

"I'm not blaming anyone. I certainly don't mind being tied up with you."

His brows rose. "Oh. You don't, huh?"

When Jackson leaned in for another kiss, Serena pressed her hand to his chest. "How about you hold that thought until later?"

"Later?" He started to frown but then his eyes widened as he caught her true intention. A broad smile lit up his face. "I think that can be arranged."

More and more people continued to arrive at the market. No wonder Gizmo had changed his mind about wandering off and instead wanted to be held. He was not used to such a crowd. The Christmas market really drew in the people. But who could blame them? This was the most wonderful time of the year.

Jackson quickly untangled all three of them. "There. Now shall we go explore?"

"Are you sure you're up for this? The doctor did say that your leg will tire quickly with that boot on."

"Stop worrying. I'm fine. I'll let you know when I get tired."

"You promise."

"I do."

"What about Gizmo?"

"Let him walk for a bit. That pup has more energy than anyone I know. And then when we get home, he'll sleep instead of getting into more mischief."

"That sounds like a good plan." She smiled up at him. "I like the way you think."

"Well, if you like that wait until you find out what I have planned for later."

She couldn't help but laugh at his outrageous flirting. Things between them were so much different now—so much easier since he knew the truth about her. If only she had known how good it could be between them, she would have told him sooner.

They strolled through the Christmas market locally known as Christkindlmarkt. The thing Serena loved most was sampling all of the local delicacies—from sipping mulled wine to devouring *kiachl*, somewhat like a donut with cranberry jam. Serena had never tasted anything so delightful. Jackson enjoyed the *raclette brot*, a type of bread with warm cheese. And of course Gizmo had to sample most everything, too. So much for her rule about not feeding him human food. After all, it was the holidays. Everyone deserved a treat.

"Are you enjoying yourself?" Jackson asked.

"I am." In the background a brass band played holiday tunes. And overhead, strands of white twinkle lights brightened the night sky. "This place is amazing. And I can't bring myself to stop sampling all of the delicacies."

"I know what you mean. I'm full, but I just have to try one more thing."

They both laughed. The evening was perfect. No one recognized her with her strawberry blonde hair pulled up in a ponytail and lack of makeup. Here in Austria, she was just another person on the arm of a very handsome gentleman.

And then he reached out and took her hand in his. His fingers threaded through hers quickly and naturally as though they'd been doing it for years. Her heart leaped in her chest.

This man, he was something extraordinary.

And Serena knew in that moment, in the middle of the Christmas market, that her life would never be the same.

He couldn't stop smiling.

Jackson sat in the passenger seat as Serena pulled into the driveway of the cabin. She'd chatted the whole way home from the Christmas market. He was glad he'd suggested they go. Not only was it a scouting mission for his segment for his morning news show, but it also had been their first official date.

Serena put the vehicle in Park and turned off the engine. "And we're home."

"Hey, what happened to your smile?"

She shrugged. "It's just that all of the magic of the evening disappeared."

"Ouch." He grasped at his chest.

"What's the matter? What hurts?"

"My ego. You just pierced it. I'm wounded."

"Oh." She smacked his shoulder. "You had me worried. I thought something was seriously wrong with you."

"There is. You just said the magic has ended."

"You know what I meant. The music. The festive mood. The amazing food. I loved the evening."

"And you don't think my company can compare?"

Serena's green eyes widened. "What exactly are you implying?"

"Forget twinkle lights, I'm thinking of setting off some fireworks tonight."

Her mouth lifted into a smile that made her eyes sparkle. "I don't know. Do you think you're up to it?"

"Let me give you a preview." He leaned forward and pressed his lips to hers.

His kiss was gentle and restrained. He wouldn't push her, but he needed to extend the invitation. It'd been a very long time since he was with a woman. His gut tightened at the thought of living up to Serena's expectations.

But he didn't have long to contemplate because she kissed him back with undeniable desire, which soothed his worries. As their kiss deepened, a warmth flooded his chest. The cracks and crevices in his heart filled in. In that moment, he no longer felt like a shell of a man. He felt complete and eager to step into the next stage of his life. Whatever that may be.

Serena pulled back. "We should go inside. It's getting cold out here."

They both turned to find out why Gizmo wasn't whining to go inside. The pup was sound asleep in the back seat. Jackson couldn't help but smile.

"So he really does run out of energy once in a while."

"It's hard to believe, but it does happen. Isn't he so cute?"

"He is...when he's sleeping."

"Hey." She swatted at Jackson's arm. Then a worried look crossed over her face. "You do like Gizmo, don't you?"

He knew by the serious tone of her voice that him bonding with her dog was nonnegotiable. Someday she'd make a good mother. Unlike his mother who'd taken his dog away from him.

"Oh, no," she said. "You don't like him."

"What? No. I mean, yes, I do."

"But you frowned when I asked you about it."

"That wasn't why I was frowning. I swear. I didn't even realize I was frowning."

He was going to have to do better to keep his thoughts from being so obvious on his face. Considering his job, he was normally quite adept at it. But either Serena could read him better than most or he felt so at ease around her that he didn't think to hide anything.

And now he had no choice but to share with Serena that painful moment in his childhood. He'd never told anyone about it—not even his wife. It was a part of his life that he'd blocked out—until he'd met Serena and Gizmo.

"I was just thinking about the past. I had a dog once. He was rambunctious and I was young, about seven years old. Long story short, he got in lots of trouble and a week later, my mother took him back to the pound."

He remembered clearly how his mother had told him to stop crying. He wasn't a sniveling wimp. If he was strong, if he was a man—unlike his father who ran off at the first sign of trouble—then Jackson would be fine. He didn't need a dog.

He'd been so young at the time that his priority was not letting his mother down. He wanted her to be proud of him more than anything else in the world—even more than having his puppy.

"I can't believe it," Serena said. "Your mom took your dog away."

He nodded. "But it's okay."

"What's okay about it? She got it for you, but seven days later she took it back to the shelter."

"It was my fault. I didn't take care of Rover like I'd promised."

"You were only seven. How responsible can a seven-year-old be?"

Jackson shrugged, realizing that even after all this time he was protecting his mother. "It doesn't matter. It was a long time ago."

"But it still bothers you, so it matters."

He pulled back and reached for the door handle. "I don't want to talk about this."

Serena didn't say anything as he walked away. By the rigid line of his shoulders, she knew the evening had been ruined. And it had held such promise.

CHAPTER TWELVE

WHAT HAD HAPPENED?

Serena had been trying to make sense of what had happened to their perfect evening ever since Jackson had withdrawn from her. That had been last night and now, not quite twenty-four hours later, he was still unusually quiet.

Had she misread everything last night?

Impossible. There was no way she'd misread his kisses—his very stirring kisses. Those kisses had left promises of more to come. Oh, he had been into her just as much as she had been into him. So where had it all gone so wrong?

Or was it for the best to put a halt to their desires? After all, every man that she'd let get close had hurt her. Why should Jackson be any different?

But the truth was, she wanted him to be different. She wanted him to be the exception to everything she knew about men—that they were critical, careless with their words and didn't believe in love for love's sake but rather for what it could do for them and their careers.

"Hey, what has you so deep in thought?" Jackson's deep voice stirred her.

At last he was talking to her. A smile came to her face. Maybe she was making too big a deal of things. Perhaps he'd just been tired last night. After all, the doctor did say that the boot on his ankle would tire him out.

"I was just thinking about what I'm working on."

"I'm sorry to interrupt." Jackson had a mug in each hand and held one out to her. "I just thought you might like this."

"Oh, coffee. I always like coffee."

"It's not coffee."

"It isn't?" She accepted the mug and glanced into it to find little marshmallows and hot chocolate. "Thank you."

"I just thought that with it snowing again this might be fitting."

"It is." She took a sip of the milky chocolate. It was perfect. "This is the best hot chocolate I've ever had."

He smiled proudly. "Thank you."

"Is this from a packet? If so, I have to make a note to buy some when I get back to the States."

He shook his head. "It isn't from a box. I made it."

She took another sip and moaned in pleasure. "How did you make it?"

He eyed her up as though trying to decide if he should divulge the information. "Can you keep a secret?"

"Definitely. I just have to be able to make this again. It's that good."

"Well, while we were at the Christmas market yesterday, I bought some chocolate."

"Why don't I remember this?"

"Because you and Gizmo were at the stall with the gourmet dog biscuits. Anyway, that's my secret."

"So you melted chocolate into milk."

"Not just any chocolate but dark chocolate. However, you can't tell anyone. It's our secret."

She smiled, liking the idea that they shared confidences. "I can't believe you are so good in the kitchen." And then she realized that he might not take her words as a compliment. "It's just that you are so busy. I don't know how you find the time."

"I don't have a busy social calendar, not anymore. Anyway, once you learn how to cook, it's like riding a bike, you never forget."

"I wouldn't know."

"You mean you can't ride a bike?" The look on his face was one of unimaginable horror.

"No. I mean, yes, I can ride a bike. It's the cooking that I never conquered."

"Did you ever try?"

She nodded. "I've attempted to teach myself without success. My mother can't cook, so she obviously didn't show me. And my father thought that cooking was a waste of time. That's what he paid people to do. So he forbade me from spending time in the kitchen when instead I could spend the time taking voice lessons as well as dance and acting classes."

"Sounds like you had a very busy and educational childhood."

She shrugged. "It was what it was." Her childhood was a mixed bag of extravagance and neglect. She was certain she wasn't the only Hollywood child to have the same experience. "How did you become so good in the kitchen?"

"Come to the kitchen with me and I'll tell you."

"The kitchen, but why?"

"Because you're going to have your first cooking lesson."

She struggled to keep her mouth from gaping. After she recovered from her surprise, she said, "You don't want to do this. I'm pretty sure I can burn water if left alone."

He smiled. "I think you're better than you give yourself credit for."

"I wouldn't be so certain."

"Come on." He reached out and took her free hand. He tugged until she got to her feet. "After all, you can make chili."

"You know that it was out of a can."

"Still, you didn't burn it. That's a start."

"I must admit that I can handle a microwave."

"Good." They moved to the kitchen. "Now you have to pick—red or white?"

"Wine?"

"No. Sauce."

She liked them both. "Paired with what?"

"Pasta and..." He opened the freezer and searched inside. "How do you feel about shrimp?"

"I love it." She was so thankful that he'd given up on the idea of teaching her to cook. She was hopeless. But with Jackson cooking, this was going to be a delicious dinner.

"Good. Now what sauce would you prefer?"

"White." She couldn't help but smile. She'd never been in the kitchen with a man where his sole interest was in preparing her dinner. In fact, no man had ever cooked her dinner. Her smile broadened.

"Well, what are you doing standing over there. Put your hot cocoa down and wash up. You have work to do."

"Me? Cook?" This was not a good idea. Not at all.

"Uh-huh. In fact, you can do it all yourself. I'll supervise."

Her stomach plummeted. So much for the delicious dinner that she'd been envisioning. "Are you sure you want to ruin dinner? I'm good with watching."

"You'll never learn to cook that way. Trust me. This will work."

She had absolutely no illusions about this cooking adventure turning out to be anything but a disaster. Still, it was sweet that Jackson wanted to help her. She just hated the thought of disappointing him.

Why exactly did he elect himself to teach Serena to cook?

Because it was easier than discussing his background. That was one thing about June, she never prodded him for answers. But Serena was the exact opposite. She was most definitely the curious sort. He wasn't sure how to deal with her.

For so long now, he'd been fine with leaving the past alone. But being around Serena had him reexamining his life. It all made him uncomfortable. The more he thought about things, the more he questioned his choices.

He didn't like the uneasiness filling him. Before he'd arrived in Austria, he'd had a plan—a focus. His life was to revolve around his work. Now he didn't know if that was the right path for him.

What he needed now was to get away from here—away from Serena. He'd be able to think clearly and he could go back to—to what? His lonely condo in New York? His workaholic tendencies?

No matter what his life may be lacking, it was better than the alternative—loving and losing. Once down that road was enough for him. He was better off alone.

He shoved all these thoughts and questions into the box at the back of his mind. Tomorrow his camera crew would arrive. And he doubted that his life would ever intersect Serena's again. Although, the thought of not seeing her again settled heavy in his chest.

"Where do I start?" Serena's voice jarred him from his thoughts.

"You'll need to rinse the shrimp under some water and remove the tails. And while you do that, I'll put on a pot of water for the pasta."

He couldn't believe that no one had ever taken the time to teach her to cook. He felt bad for her. It made him wonder what kind of a childhood she'd had.

"Were you left alone a lot as a child?" The question was out of his mouth before he realized that it was none of his business. He placed the pot on the burner and turned the heat to high. "Never mind, you don't have to answer that."

She glanced over at him. "Is this my friend Jackson asking or is it Jackson Bennett, king of the morning shows, who wants to know?"

Ouch! That comment hurt more than he was expecting. "I promise nothing you share with me will show up on my show or in the press. I'd like to be your friend."

She rinsed off another handful of colossal shrimp and set them aside before she turned back to him. "I'd like that. It's just that I never had anyone in my life that I could completely trust."

"That must have been rough."

She shrugged. "I dealt with it. I learned pretty quick that I could only count on myself."

"Still, that's not right. A kid should have someone to turn to—someone to rely on."

Serena arched a brow. "Are we talking about me or you?"

Jackson realized that he'd let his emotions get away from him. It was just that he felt a strong connection with Serena. It was something that he'd never felt with June or anyone else in his life.

He cleared his throat. "Why don't I give you a hand?"

He moved next to her at the sink and started removing the tails of the shrimp. Why did he keep opening himself up to her? He knew better. The real Jackson Bennett was a man with flaws and scars. He would never add up to the vision she gained from watching him on television.

Serena was used to men who had it all together—looks, careers and charisma. He was the shell of the man he used to be. Cancer had more victims than those carrying the disease. It could suck life right out of the people around it—grinding hopes and dreams into smithereens. And sometimes leaving in its wake a broken person.

"Do you cook a lot?" Serena asked.

He shrugged as he swallowed hard. "As much as I can. It's the only way I've found to make sure that I fit into my suits." He reached for a couple cloves of garlic. "Eating out is tempting, but then I start putting on the pounds that I can't lose even when I go to the gym."

"I totally get that. They say the camera puts on ten pounds but that was before high definition. Now it adds fifteen pounds and amplifies any wrinkles or blemishes. So if you can show me an easier way to watch the scale, I'm all for it."

Jackson placed a clove of garlic on a cutting

board. He showed her how to put the flat side of a chef's knife on the clove and with her palm press down on it to remove the skin. She did the same with the other clove. Then Serena minced the garlic before chopping some fresh parsley and tomatoes that they'd picked up at the market.

"Jackson?"

He'd just added butter to the skillet. "Yes?"

"I thought I was supposed to cook the meal."

She was right. He'd just gotten so caught up in his thoughts of the past that he'd been moving around the kitchen on automatic. "You're right. Sorry. It's just habit." He stepped to the side of the stove. "Okay, then. Here. Take the handle. You'll want to swish it so the butter coats the bottom of the pan."

She did as he said.

"Now add the garlic." He talked her through the process of adding the shrimp, the fresh parsley and a little seasoning. Jackson inhaled the savory aroma. "Smells wonderful."

He added the angel-hair pasta to the pot of boiling water, gave it a stir and lowered the temperature.

"You're cheating," Serena said.

And then he realized he should have let her do all the steps. "But it's so much easier when we work as a team. Trust me, you're doing the hard part."

"What do I do next?"

"Turn the shrimp."

He hovered just over her shoulder, watching her every move. He told himself that he was just trying to be an attentive mentor, but the truth was he was drawn to Serena like a magnet. There was something so appealing about her and it went far deeper than her natural beauty. There was a tenderness—a vulnerability— about her. And she made him feel as though he were her equal—as though they were perfectly matched for each other.

"Jackson." Serena waved a hand in front of him to gain his attention. "The shrimp's pink."

Pulled back from his thoughts, he blinked and quickly took stock of where dinner stood. He told her to drain the shrimp and set them aside. Then they added more butter, flour, milk, chicken broth and seasoning to the pan. Then the most important part—the cheese. She added lots of mozzarella and Parmesan. In the meantime, Jackson drained the pasta.

They worked well together. Really well. It was like they'd been doing it all their lives. And he wasn't sure what to make of it. Perhaps he'd isolated himself too much since his wife's death and now he was overreacting to Serena's presence.

Oh, who was he kidding? He was falling for

this woman—this award-winning actress. And he had no idea what to do about it.

"Do I add the tomatoes now?" she asked.

"Yes. And the shrimp. And make sure you remove it from the heat."

He wasn't sure where this evening was headed, but he sure was hungry now. And his hunger had absolutely nothing to do with the amazing Alfredo shrimp pasta they'd just created.

CHAPTER THIRTEEN

DINNER HAD BEEN PERFECT.

The company was amazing.

Jackson couldn't recall the last time he'd had such a wonderful evening. And now Serena leaned back on the couch with Gizmo on one side of her and Jackson on the other. The glow of the fireplace added a romantic ambience to the room. And when Jackson settled his arm around her, she didn't resist.

Was it wrong that he wanted this night with her? He knew that it would be a fleeting moment. After all, he was going to head back to New York as soon as his work was completed.

But there was something special between them. He wasn't ready to put a label on it. Not yet.

"And what has you so deep in thought?" Jackson asked, noticing he wasn't the only one staring reflectively into the fire.

"I don't know."

"It wouldn't happen to be that masterpiece you've been working on every spare moment you get, would it?"

"You'll laugh if I tell you."

Jackson pulled back so he could look at her. "Why do you think I would do that?"

She shrugged. "It's what has happened in the past."

"Not by me."

"True." Serena worried her bottom lip. "I shouldn't have said that. You've been so kind to me, helping me in the kitchen and visiting the Christmas market even though you really didn't feel up to it. Those are things other men in my life would never have done. I shouldn't have made such a thoughtless remark."

"It's okay." He once again settled next to her.

"Can I have a do-over?" When he nodded, she said, "I was thinking about my script."

"You're writing a television show?" He wanted to know more about her. Everything about her fascinated him. "Have you always been a writer?"

Serena didn't say anything. He willed her to open up to him because she was like a mystery. The more he knew about her, the more he wanted to learn.

Her gaze met his. "I've always been a reader. When I was younger, I would write, but then my father found out and told me that I was wasting my time."

"I'm sorry he smashed your dreams."

She shrugged. "I shouldn't have let him. But I was young and easily swayed."

"I take it you're not so easily swayed these days."

"I'd like to think not. Time and experience have a way of changing a person."

"And in your case, I think you've made the most of your experiences."

She arched a brow at him. "You think you know me that well?"

A small smile teased his lips. "I think you are an amazing woman with a big heart. You love your puppy and you take in injured strangers."

Color rushed to her face. He couldn't believe someone as beautiful as her hadn't been complimented on a regular basis. But he couldn't deny that she was adorable with the rosy hue in her cheeks. Not that he was thinking of starting anything serious with her.

It was time he changed the subject before he said too much and made them both uncomfortable. "So what are you writing? A family saga? Or a paranormal series?"

"No...ah, actually, it's a big-screen movie." She paused as though expecting him to say something, but he quietly waited for her to finish. "A family saga with a central romance."

"That's great."

"You're just saying that."

"No. I'm not. I read some every day. Mostly biographies but I also enjoy some suspense. I think anyone that writes has a precious gift."

This time she shifted on the couch until she could look him in the eyes. "Do you mean that?"

"I do. I'd like to read it, if you'd let me."

She shook her head and sat back on the couch. "You can't. It's not finished."

"How about when it's finished?"

"That's the thing. I'm stuck. I've tried different endings but nothing I've tried seems to work."

"Give it time. Don't force yourself. If you relax, the answer will come to you."

"Do you really believe that?"

"I do. It works for me. When I'm working on a segment. I like to do a lot of my own writing."

"Thanks." She turned her head and smiled at him. "I really appreciate your support."

He lowered his voice. "Just know that you can always talk to me—about anything. I care about you."

Serena's heart jumped into her throat. She turned her head to say something, but words failed her. Her gaze met his dark eyes. He wanted her. It was right there in his eyes. They were filled with desire.

When he lowered his head, she found her lips were just inches from his. Her heart beat faster. Should she do it? Should she make the next move? Meet him halfway?

Perhaps actions did actually speak louder than words. She leaned forward, claiming his lips with her own. They were smooth, warm and oh, so inviting.

Jackson shifted on the couch so that he was cupping her face. Her arms instinctively wrapped around his neck. The kiss deepened. There was no hesitation—no tentativeness. There was only passion and desire.

It seemed so right for them to be together. It was like she'd been looking for him all of her life. He accepted her as she was and he hadn't tried to change her.

Jackson leaned back on the couch, pulling her on top of him. Her hands shifted to his chest. Beneath her fingers she felt his strapping muscles. Her heart fluttered in her chest as her body tingled all over. She'd never felt this way with a man before—not even close.

Thoughts of Jackson's approaching departure crowded into her head, but she forcefully shoved them away. If all she had after this vacation were memories, she wanted them to be good ones. She wanted them to be so good that she would recall them with a smile when she was a little old lady.

She was beginning to realize the greatest gifts in life were the good memories. She wanted to make exceptional memories with Jackson. She needed him to remember her, because she would never ever forget him. Not a chance.

Jackson took the lead with their kiss. Exploring, taunting and teasing. Her body pulsed with lust and desire. Beneath her palm, his heart beat hard and fast. Oh, yeah, this was going to be an unforgettable night—

Something cold and wet pressed to her cheek. *What in the world?*

Serena pulled back to find Gizmo standing up on his back legs with his nose next to hers. A curious look reflected in his eyes as though he was thinking: *What did I miss? Huh? Huh?*

Simultaneously Serena and Jackson let out a laugh. Gizmo looking pleased with himself.

"Arff! Arff!"

With a smile on his face, Jackson said, "I think we should take this into the bedroom."

Serena's gaze moved between her two favorite males. "I think you're right."

Once they got Gizmo settled on his dog bed, Jackson took her hand in his. She led him to the bedroom where they could explore these kisses in private.

CHAPTER FOURTEEN

SERENA COULDN'T SLEEP.

She was too wound up—too happy.

For a while now, she'd been watching Jackson sleep. His face was so handsome and he looked so peaceful. He was so much more than the alpha image he projected on television. There was a gentleness to him—a compassion that broke through the wall around her heart.

This evening had been more amazing than she'd ever thought possible. And as she watched Jackson draw in one deep breath after the other, she had a light-bulb moment. She realized the reason she couldn't finish her screenplay.

Her mind started to play over where she'd left her heroine bereft after the black moment with the hero. Until now, everything Serena had tried to bring the couple back together had felt hollow and empty. And that was because she didn't know what it was like to fall in love.

Until now…

She was falling in love with Jackson Bennett—the man who greeted America with a smile and a mug of coffee every weekday.

And he was the inspiration she'd needed to finish the script. Perhaps this was a whole new start to her life. She knew that she was jumping too far ahead and she had to slow down.

After all, Jackson had said that he cared about her—not that he loved her or that he was falling in love with her. Maybe that was the line he handed all his women. She didn't want to believe it because he just didn't seem like the type to go casually from one relationship to the next.

Was that how her heroine would feel? Or would she be confident that they could overcome their biggest obstacle? The questions continued to whirl through her mind, but she kept them relegated to her script. She would figure out where her relationship with Jackson went later—preferably after she got some sleep.

But for now, she had a mission. She gently slipped out of bed. There was a distinct nip in the air. She threw on clothes as fast as she could. All the while she kept glancing over her shoulder to make sure she hadn't disturbed Jackson. His breathing was deep and even.

Holding her breath, she tiptoed out of the room, closing the door behind her. The fire had died off in the great room and a definite chill was in the air. Gizmo lifted his head and looked at her. He didn't make any attempt to move from his oversize cushion with his blue blanket and his stuffed teddy he used for a pillow. She turned on a lamp next to the couch. Gizmo gave her a curious look as she made her way to the fireplace to rekindle the fire. But apparently it was too cold or he was too tired to beg her to take him outside. She couldn't blame him.

With the fire started, she fussed over Gizmo before gathering her laptop and moving to the end of the couch closest to the fireplace. With a throw blanket over her legs, she opened her laptop and set to work. For the first time in quite a while, her fingers moved rapidly over the keyboard. When the words came to her without a lot of effort, it was like magic. It was as though the story had taken on a life of its own. The characters were speaking to her and all she had to do was type out the words.

She didn't know how much time had passed but the sun was just starting to come up when she typed *The End* and pressed Save for the last time. She shut her laptop, set it on the coffee table and then laid her head on the backrest of the couch with a satisfied smile, her heavy eyelids drooping closed.

* * *

Quack. Quack.

Jackson's eyes opened at the sound of his alarm. His assistant, who was fresh out of college, had decided to play a trick on him and had reset his phone to various obnoxious sounds. A duck for his alarm, an old car horn for his phone and other random, off-the-wall sounds. What she didn't count on was him liking them. They were easy to distinguish from everyone else's cell phone. And best of all, it made those around him smile. So he'd left the tones as they were.

He wondered what Serena thought of his quacking alarm. He opened an eye and glanced over to find the bed empty. Serena was gone. He ran his hand over the pillow and mattress, finding her spot cold. Apparently she'd been gone for quite some time.

He sat up and looked around the room, but there was no sign of her. What did her absence mean? Did she regret their lovemaking? Did he regret it?

The reality of their actions sharpened his sleep-hazed thoughts. He'd made love to another woman. He sunk back against the pillows. Maybe it was a good thing that Serena had gone. He wasn't sure he'd be good company right now.

He'd broken his word to himself. He was moving forward—starting something—leaving the memories of his wife behind. Guilt slugged him in the gut. What would June think?

No. He couldn't go there. Right now, he had to straighten things out with Serena. He had to tell her that they'd made a mistake. But if Serena hadn't spent the entire night, did that mean she wasn't looking for a relationship? Could it be that easy?

The only way to find the answer was to find Serena. He quickly showered and dressed. His film crew was picking him up this morning. And while out and about, he'd arranged to rent another vehicle that he'd pick up some time that day.

He exited the master suite and Gizmo came running up to him. "Shh..."

Gizmo moved to the front door. Jackson glanced around, expecting Serena to be hot on Gizmo's heels, but she was nowhere to be found. Jackson grabbed his coat and the leash. Gizmo was so excited that he kept stepping in front of Jackson, almost tripping him.

"Arff!"

A distinct grunt soon followed.

Jackson put his finger to his lips. "Shh..."

Gizmo's tail continued to rapidly swish.

Jackson tiptoed over to the couch and there he found Serena curled up in a ball beneath a little blanket that didn't even completely cover her. She'd rather freeze on the couch than be snug in bed with him?

The thought dug at him as he rushed to the bedroom to grab a blanket from the bed. He draped it over her. With a sigh, she snuggled to it.

Jackson stared down at her very sweet face. She looked almost angelic as she slept. He wondered what she was dreaming about. He doubted that it would be about him. Not that he wanted her to dream of him.

No matter what Serena said, she still didn't trust him. Her sleeping out here was proof of it. And why should she when he acted without thinking? He had nothing to offer her.

"Arff!"

He had to take Gizmo out before Serena woke. It would be so much easier if they didn't speak—not just yet. He had to get his thoughts sorted. He needed time to find the right words to say to her—to salvage their friendship. Serena was a very special person and he hated the thought of completely losing her from his life.

CHAPTER FIFTEEN

THE CABIN WAS QUIET—too quiet.

Serena utilized the printer on the desk in the great room and spent most of the day proofing her script. But the reason she'd rushed in and immersed herself in editing the script had more to do with filling in the silence around her. She was amazed at how quickly she'd gotten used to having Jackson around. And how much she missed him when he was gone.

Warning bells rang in her head. She was getting in deep—perhaps too deep. It wasn't like Jackson was asking for her hand in marriage. Not that she wanted him to drop down on one knee. She just wanted to know that he cared for her—and his feelings for her were more than a passing fancy.

Her gaze moved toward the window. Evening was settling in and snow had begun to fall. Big fat flakes fluttered about before piling on top of the many feet of snow. And Jackson was out there somewhere on these mountain roads. She wished he'd taken the four-wheel drive like she'd insisted. But he'd assured her that he would be fine. If he was so fine—why wasn't he home yet?

She gathered the pages she'd been working on and put a rubber band around them. With a deep breath and a bit of trepidation, she carried the script into the master suite. Jackson had requested to read it. Why should she resist him? After all, if she wanted it to be produced into a movie, a lot of other people would have to read it.

She stopped in front of the king-size bed. She lowered the pages that she'd been clutching to her chest. The pages still had her corrections on them, but they were clean enough for Jackson to read.

Her gaze moved to the title page. Letting Jackson read this would be more revealing than making love to him—at least that was the way it felt in that moment. They weren't just words on a page, they were an intimate piece of her. Her empty stomach roiled. She swallowed hard.

Without giving it any further thought, she placed the manuscript at the end of the bed. Then she turned and headed for the door as fast as her legs would carry her. She knew that if she didn't leave quickly she would chicken out and take back the pages.

Just then a set of headlights streamed in through the windows. Jackson was home. She smiled and Gizmo ran to the door barking.

"It looks like I'm not the only one anxious to see Jackson, huh, boy?"

Gizmo turned to her and wagged his tail before he turned back to the door to continue barking.

Serena glanced at the clock on the fireplace mantel. She would have to let the little furbaby get the first greeting. She was needed in the kitchen. She'd prepared dinner to the best of her ability and it was just about to come out of the oven.

Time to get it over with.

Jackson had played out this scene in his mind more times than he cared to admit. None of it ended well. But he couldn't put it off any longer.

He opened the door, not sure what to expect. Gizmo jumped up on him with his tail swishing back and forth. Jackson had him get down so that he could step inside and close the door.

Then Jackson bent over to pet Gizmo's fuzzy head. "Hey, boy, I'm happy to see you, too."

Maybe he should reconsider getting a dog. It was really nice to come home to somebody.

But it was Serena that he wanted to see. Where was she?

He'd been thinking of what to say to her all day, to the point where he'd been distracted during taping. It'd made for a very long day with many retakes. And he'd ended up frustrating his crew. He'd apologized and blamed it on his ankle. He wasn't ready to tell anyone about Serena. They'd make more of the situation than he wanted.

He'd just shrugged off his coat and hung it near the door to dry when he heard footsteps behind him. He turned and there was Serena looking all down-to-earth in faded jeans, a red sweater and her hair pulled up in a ponytail.

There was something different about her. It took him a moment and then he realized that she'd changed her hair back to its former blond color—at least close to it.

"You changed your hair?"

She smiled and nodded. "I thought it was time that I got back to being me."

He didn't know what that meant. Did it have something to do with her creeping out of his bed during the night? Was she sending him some sort of message? If so, he wasn't sure he understood.

"It looks nice." That was not what he'd planned to say, but he was caught off guard.

"And you are just in time."

"For what?"

"Dinner. I cooked again."

"Oh. Okay." Why was she acting all nice? He thought she would be angry at him for rushing things last night. Instead, she was cooking for him. What had he missed?

"Don't look so worried. It came out of a box and I followed the directions." She sent him a puzzled look as though she didn't understand why he was acting strange. "I set the table in the kitchen, but we can eat in here if you'd prefer."

"Serena, stop it."

Her eyes widened. "Stop what?"

"Acting all nice. Like nothing happened."

"Oh. You mean last night."

"Yes, last night. Don't act like you forgot."

"How could I forget?"

At last, they were getting somewhere. "Well, say it."

"Say what?"

Was she going to make this whole thing difficult? Was he going to have to drag every word out of her mouth? One thing was for sure, if he didn't know it before, he knew it now, Serena was so different from June. When June was angry, he knew it. With the outside world, his wife had been reserved. With him, not so much. Thankfully they hadn't argued much.

But Serena for some reason was masking her displeasure. Instead of telling him the problem, she was hiding behind a friendly but cool demeanor. He didn't like it. He'd rather face the problem and then move on. So if she wasn't going to do something about it, he would.

"Say what you're upset about. Don't hide it."

She worried her bottom lip. "That's strange, because I'm usually a much better actress. It's nothing for you to worry about."

"Of course I'm worried. It involves me." He stopped himself just short of saying that if there was a way he could make it up to her he would.

That was how he used to handle June. Then again, maybe that was how June handled him. He wasn't so sure anymore. The more time he spent with Serena, the more clarity he was gaining on his past. Maybe it hadn't been as perfect as he wanted to remember.

She sighed. "I don't want it to ruin dinner. We can talk after we eat."

He did not understand this woman. She wanted to eat first and then argue? Who did things like that? Before he could ask her, she'd headed into the kitchen.

He sighed and shook his head. He might as well as get comfortable. This was going to be a long evening. He headed for the master suite to take off his suit jacket and tie.

When he entered the room, he flipped on the overhead light. He kicked off his shoes and loosened his tie. He really didn't have any appetite. He'd been tied up in knots all day.

He sat down on the bed and his hand landed on paper. He glanced down to find a ream of paper. He picked it up and read the top sheet: *Life Atop The Ferris Wheel* by Mae Ellwood.

Jackson removed the rubber band and flipped to the last page. The last line read: *The End*. She'd finished it? But last night she'd said she was stuck.

He dropped the pages to the bed and headed for the kitchen. He plowed through the door and came to a stop when he found the kitchen aglow with a candle in the center. Dishes were set out and dinner was awaiting him. But it was the woman wearing the great big smile that drew and held his attention.

"Dinner's ready. I hope you brought your appetite."

"I, uh, sure." But he couldn't eat, not yet. There was one thing he had to know. "Did you get out of bed last night to go work on your script?"

The smile slipped from her face. "Is that what's bothering you?"

"Of course it is. Imagine how I felt when I woke up alone and the spot next to me was cold, as in you never slept there."

She approached him. "I'm sorry. I didn't think. Well, actually I did a lot of thinking. That's why I couldn't go to sleep. I realized what I was missing for the ending of the script and I had to go write it out while it was fresh in my mind. I was afraid that if I went to sleep I would forget parts of it."

He breathed his first easy breath all day. "So you didn't leave because you regretted what happened between us?"

The smile returned to her face. "No, silly. I don't regret any of it."

He reached out and drew her to him. She melted into his embrace as though they'd been doing it for years. He planted a kiss on her lips. She immediately kissed him back.

As his lips moved over hers, each muscle in his body began to relax. He had no idea until now how worked up he'd been. And it'd all been over a screenplay.

Serena pressed a hand to his chest and pulled back. "Are you ready to eat?"

He really didn't want to eat at the moment. He'd be more than happy to keep kissing her. But he knew this meal was a big deal. And he was proud of her for going outside her comfort zone and cooking dinner—even if it came out of a box.

"Sure. What is it?"

"It's baked mac-'n'-cheese. Is that all right?"

"Sure."

"And there was some bread that I picked up at the market."

"Sounds good to me." After they were settled at the table, Jackson said, "So I saw the manuscript on the bed. Did you leave that for me?"

She nodded. "Did you change your mind about reading it?"

"Definitely not." He took her hand in his. "Thank you for trusting me with it."

"Thank you for caring enough to read it."

Tonight Serena would sleep and he'd stay up. He loved to read and the fact that Serena had penned this script made it all the more special. No matter how much he tried to deny it, Serena was special. He just didn't know what to do about his growing feelings for her and his nagging guilt over letting go of his past.

CHAPTER SIXTEEN

THE FOLLOWING EVENING, Serena paced back and forth in the great room. Gizmo was right behind her, pacing, too. Back and forth they went, from the staircase to the front door. If she stopped, Gizmo stopped. He always did sense when something was bothering her.

She stopped and looked down at the dog, who sat down and looked up at her. "What are we going to do? We can't keep pacing. It's not helping anything."

"Arff!"

"Sorry. I'm too worked up to sit."

If only she had something to take her mind off Jackson's impending critique of her script. But now that the script was done, she didn't have anything else planned for the trip. If only she knew how to knit or crochet, she'd have something to do with her hands.

Instead, all she could do was wonder if Jackson had liked the story line. He'd left that morning while she'd still been asleep. And now he was home, but he hadn't even mentioned one word about the script. He could have at least given her a clue if he liked what he'd read so far.

Jackson exited the kitchen.

Serena stopped pacing. Instead of barraging him with questions about her script, she calmly asked, "Do you need help with dinner?"

"No. It's all under control."

Should she ask the question that was teetering on the tip of her tongue? But what if he didn't like it? What if he hated it? Her stomach plummeted.

Forgetting that he was still in the room, she resumed pacing. In time, hopefully the activity would work out some of her nervous tension. Because she'd resolved not to ask Jackson about the script. She would not. It was for the best.

"Anything on your mind?" Jackson asked.

She stopped and looked at him. Was he reading her mind? Or was this his way of toying with her? Well, she wasn't falling for it.

"No," she said as normally as possible. "Is it time to eat?"

"Actually it won't be ready for a while. I thought we could do something in the meantime."

Her gaze narrowed. "What did you have in mind?"

"You'll see. Dress warm. We're going outside."

She didn't know what he was up to, but it obviously had nothing to do with her script. "Don't you have something else you need to do?"

He paused as though considering her question. "Hmm…the meat is marinating. The potatoes are prepped. And the salad is ready. No. I have everything done."

She frowned at him. How could he forget about her script? Was it that forgettable? Disappointment settled in her chest. "Maybe you have something to read?"

A smile pulled at his very kissable lips. "I don't have anything urgent—"

"Jackson!" Every bit of her patience had been used up.

"Oh. You mean your script?" he said it innocently enough, but the smile on his face said that he'd been playing with her this whole time.

"Of course I mean the manuscript. I thought you wanted to read it."

"I did."

"You did? You mean read the whole thing already? I just gave it to you last night."

"I know. And it's your fault that I didn't get any sleep."

"You stayed up all night and read it?"

He nodded, but he didn't say a word. There

was no smile on his face. There was no clue as to what he thought of her script. He was going to make her drag it out of him.

"And…" She waved her hands as though pulling the words from him.

"And… I think…that…"

"Jackson, say it. If you hated it, just say so."

"I love it."

"What?" Surely she hadn't heard him correctly. If he loved it, why did he make it so hard for her to get an answer out of him?

"Serena, you're very talented. Your words are vivid and emotional. I could see the entire story play out in my mind."

Her heart was pounding with excitement. And a smile pulled at her lips. "Really? You're not just saying that to be nice, are you?"

"Do I look like a nice guy to you?"

"Well, yes, you do. So I have to be sure. Because if you didn't like it, you can tell me. I can take it. I might cry myself to sleep, but I can take it."

He laughed. "So much for the calm and cool Serena Winston that graces the covers of all the glossy magazines. This uncertainty and nervousness is a whole new side of you."

"Jackson!"

"Okay." The smile slipped from his face. "Yes,

I'm serious. You are a talented writer and I would like to interview you—"

"No." She didn't know how he could take such a nice compliment and ruin it in the next breath, but that was exactly what he'd done.

"You didn't even let me finish."

"You don't need to. I thought you were different. I thought you were my friend. But you're just like the others, you want something from me."

He frowned at her. "I don't know who you spend your time with, but I'm not like that. If you had let me finish, I was going to say that I could do the interview and it would be about your writing. We could start spinning the story of your screenplay and then you'd have producers and directors pounding down your door to get their hands on it."

"Oh." She wanted to believe him. She wanted to think that he wasn't after her to help further his career, but she'd trusted people in the past and they'd turned against her. "I don't think so. I want this screenplay to sell on its own merits and not the fact that I'm famous. I need to know that I can do it on my own."

His eyebrows rose. "You do know what you're turning down, don't you? I can do the interview according to your rules. I don't have to touch upon your personal life…unless you want me to."

"I... I don't know."

"Will you at least consider it?"

She sighed. "I guess. But don't get your hopes up."

"I won't. But don't dismiss the fact that you can present yourself to the world as something more than an accomplished actress."

She nodded. "I hear you. I'll consider it."

"And while you do that, I have a surprise for you. Now, go put on your warmest clothes."

"You were serious about that?" When he nodded, she asked, "What do you have in mind?"

"You'll find out as soon as you change. Hurry."

Sled riding.

Serena felt like a kid again. There was a hill beside the cabin that ended in a small field. They'd been outside for an hour. She hadn't laughed this much in a very long time, if ever. Even Gizmo was having fun riding down the hill. He took turns riding on her lap and then on Jackson's.

At first, she wasn't sure about taking Gizmo on a sled. But the hill wasn't too steep. And her pup seemed perfectly fine with it. Jackson didn't go down the hill as much as her because walking up the incline with the boot on his ankle was a hard and slow process for him. At least he'd thought ahead and had wrapped a bag around his leg to keep it dry.

Serena felt bad that he couldn't enjoy sledding as much as her, but he insisted she keep going and Gizmo had barked his agreement. Jackson had even brought along a thermos of his amazing hot chocolate. And as the sun set, she couldn't think of anyplace she'd rather be.

After they took a seat on an old log, she turned to him. "Thank you for this. Would you believe I've never been sledding before?"

"Never?"

She shook her head.

"I thought you said you went to Tahoe."

"Later. As an adult. By then I spent most of my time in the lodge." She took a sip of hot cocoa. "When I was a kid, I didn't know what snow was. My father hated it. And my mother, well, she had her own life."

"I'm sorry. I grew up in New York, so we had snow often."

"Did your parents take you sledding?"

He shook his head. "My father left when I was seven. And my mother was always working. When she wasn't working, she was blaming me for my father leaving."

"That's awful. It must have been so hard on you. I'm so sorry."

He stared off into the distance. He didn't say

anything for the longest time. She didn't push him. Maybe it was time that she opened up more about herself.

She drew in a deep breath to settle her nerves. "I know what it's like to have a rough childhood. Though most people wouldn't guess it because my family had money and fame. A lot of people think that money equates to happiness. I can testify that it doesn't. Sometimes I think the more money you have, the unhappier you are."

She chanced a glance as Jackson to see if he was listening.

Jackson cleared his throat. "My father was a doctor. But when he split, he was terrible at paying my mother what he owed her. She had to fight and beg for every check. And when they did arrive, they were always months late."

"Do you still speak to your parents?"

He shook his head. "I haven't seen my father since I was nine or ten. He remarried and that was that. As for my mother, she never did stop blaming me for her marriage breaking up. I send her a check once a month to make sure she's taken care of."

"You send her money, but you don't visit?"

"It's better that way."

"Where does your mother live now?"

"In New York."

"So you live close to each other, but you never see each other?"

Jackson turned to her. "Why are you making it out like it's all my fault? My mother could just as easily track me down. My address is on every check I send—checks that she promptly cashes."

Serena knew she probably should mind her own business and keep her thoughts to herself, but she knew what it was like to lose a parent— a parent that she had unresolved issues with.

"I understand that it's tough for you, but talking as someone who recently lost a parent, I have regrets. There are so many things that I wish I had told my father. He may have annoyed me and he may not have been the perfect parent, but he was the one that was always there for me. While my mother was off moving from one younger man to the next, my father was home every night. He cared about what I did. I didn't always agree with him—okay, I rarely agreed with him—but I believe that everything he did, he did because he loved me. He just didn't know how to tell me. As a result, I never got to thank him or tell him…" Her voice cracked with emotion. She cleared her throat. "Tell him that through it all… I loved him, too. That chance was stolen away when he had a massive heart attack. Now, all I'm left with are memories and regrets."

Jackson wrapped his arm over her shoulders and pulled her close. He leaned over and pressed a kiss to the top of her head. "Neither of us have had an easy time when it comes to family. But I'm sure your father knew that you loved him."

"Just as your mother knows that each check is your way of saying that you love her?"

"Something like that."

Serena felt as though she was finally getting through to him. She shifted so that she could look into his eyes. "Tell her. Tell your mother how you feel before it's too late."

He shook his head. "It is too late. Anything that was between us ended a long time ago."

"A parent and child's love is forever."

"Maybe in some cases. But not in ours. I'm just a reminder of how her life went wrong."

"Will you at least think about it?" She knew she had no right to ask it of him, but she didn't want him to end up with nothing but remorse. And when he did realize the error of his ways, she didn't want him to talk to a cold tombstone that couldn't talk back.

"I will, if you'll agree to that interview."

Her lips pressed together into a firm line. One thing had nothing to do with the other. Nothing at all.

"Listen," Jackson said, "I know you don't like hiding who you are. I think the real you is pretty special. Don't let people steal that away from you. Stand up for who you are and what you've created."

He made a good point. It had felt so good washing out that temporary red dye from her hair, even if it all didn't come out. But was what he was asking of her the right move? Could she trust him to do the right thing? She'd heard him talking on his phone when he didn't think she was around, and he was hungry for a big story to propel his career even higher.

The only way to know was to ask. She worried her lip. If he was on the up-and-up, he would take her question as a sign of doubt in him. And if he was stringing her along for a big story, he'd never admit it. So where did that leave her?

Her heart said to trust him. He'd never hurt her. But her mind said to be cautious. She'd been burned before by people that she thought she could trust. She wished there was an easy way to figure out whom she could trust and whom she couldn't. If her past was any indication, she wasn't a good judge of character.

Jackson's gaze met hers. "I can see that you're struggling with the decision. What if we do the interview and I give you the decision of whether to air it or not?"

In his gaze, she found honesty and so much

more. Her heart pounded out its decision, overruling her mind. Sometimes she overthought things.

She pulled off her glove and held out her hand. "You have a deal."

He removed his glove and wrapped his warm hand around hers. "It's a date. Tomorrow evening after my last day of filming, I'll have the crew stop by and film it for us."

"And they won't mind? You know, staying late and doing this?"

He smiled. "When they find out who I'll be interviewing, they'll be falling all over themselves to help out."

"But they won't tell anyone?"

"Not if you don't want them to. I've worked with this crew for a long time. They are a good bunch."

Serena thought about it for a moment. "If they could just keep it quiet until after the New Year that would be good."

He lifted her hand to his lips. "It's a deal."

He kissed the back of her hand. And then he leaned over, pressing his lips to hers. She approved of the way he sealed deals. They might have to do a lot more negotiating in the future.

CHAPTER SEVENTEEN

IN A STRANGE twist of fate, that car accident had been a blessing.

As the thought crossed his mind, Jackson wondered if he should have had the doctor examine his head as well as his ankle. But if not for the accident, he most likely never would have met Serena. Instead of looking forward to Christmas, he would be looking for ways to avoid the holiday.

Just as promised, the next evening, Jackson's crew showed up at the cabin to film the interview. Jackson wasn't sure what to expect of Serena. He knew that she was professional, but he also knew how nervous she was about her new venture into script writing.

Instead of dressing in the latest fashion and wearing her signature eye makeup, she'd dressed modestly in a cream-colored sweater and matching pants. Her blond hair was twisted in back and pinned up. Wisps of hair surrounded her face, softening the style. And though she did wear makeup, it was light and just enough to accentuate her beauty. She looked perfect.

They'd previously agreed on a list of questions and Jackson followed the script, even though it was in his nature to venture into unknown territory. But out of respect to Serena, he stuck by their agreement. That was until the very end...

"Why have you decided to make this move from in front of the cameras to a place behind the scenes?"

Serena's green eyes momentarily widened as she realized it wasn't one of the preapproved questions. But he hadn't been able to help himself. He found this question to be paramount.

Like a professional, she had taken the question in stride. "I wouldn't say this is a permanent move. I've already signed on for an upcoming movie."

"That's great. I'm sure your fans will be relieved to hear the news. I know I am." It was the truth. He loved her movies. They'd helped get him through some of the toughest days of his life after his wife died. "But what drove you to try something new?"

"Actually, writing isn't new for me. The part that is new is sharing my words with the world.

I think that writing is as close to magic as you can get—bringing life to a page. And I've found that I love putting words on the page."

And now that the interview was over, it was time Jackson worked a little magic of his own. He sent the interview over to his agent. He wanted Fred to have the interview edited and polished just the way it would be done if it were to air on *Hello America*.

His agent immediately phoned. As they talked, Fred got him to admit that if Serena did go through with releasing the interview to the public that it would help not just her but him as well. His agent begged him to release it or let him do it. Fred swore that this was what they needed to rocket Jackson past the other applicants for the national evening news spot.

Jackson told his agent to calm down. This interview wasn't for him—no matter how much his career could use the boost. He'd truly done the interview with altruistic intentions. And he'd made his agent promise to have the raw footage cut and cleaned up. Then he was to forward it back to Jackson so he could play it for Serena, who still hadn't made her mind up about airing it.

"Phone me as soon as it's finished," Jackson said to his agent.

"Are you sure we can't just use some of it?

I mean, come on, she's been missing for almost two weeks now. It's all the media is talking about."

"No. And don't you dare leak her location or you'll be fired."

His agent laughed. "You'd never do that. We've been together since the beginning—"

"Fred, I'm serious. Don't do anything that we'll both regret."

"Don't worry. I've got your back."

"And you'll get the footage back to me by tomorrow night?" Jackson really wanted to present it to Serena for Christmas. He was certain she would be so impressed by the results that she'd gladly release it.

"I'll do my best," Fred said. "But you have to realize that most people are already on Christmas holiday."

"Surely you know someone you can trust to turn this around quickly."

"Well…there is someone, but he's not cheap, especially with this being the holiday."

"Money isn't an issue."

"I'll give him a call."

"Thank you," Jackson said. "I'll owe you."

"And I'll collect." His agent laughed.

As Jackson disconnected the call, he knew that Fred would in fact collect on that favor. Usually it was to get Jackson to make an appearance at some stuffy dinner that he wouldn't want to attend. But Jackson would deal with the ramifications later.

Right now, he was feeling optimistic about the final cut of the interview. Serena was a natural in front of the camera. Her face had lit up when she was talking about her script. And he'd never had so much fun interviewing anyone.

"What has you smiling?" Serena stepped through the doorway after taking Gizmo for a short walk.

"I'm just happy, is all." He stood next to the window, staring out at the snowy evening. "Do you think it always snows this much?"

"I have no idea, but I like it. It puts me in the holiday spirit." The smile slipped from her face. "I suppose now that your work is done here you'll have to head back to the States."

He reached out and wrapped his arms around her waist. "Are you saying you're already tired of me?"

"I could never get tired of you. I was just wishing you could stay for Christmas. After all, it's just in two days."

"That soon?" When she nodded, he said, "Well, if you were to twist my arm, I might consider staying. After all, my flight isn't until the day after Christmas."

Instead of smiling, she frowned.

"What's the matter?" he asked. "I thought you wanted me to stay."

"I do. That's not it. I just realized that I don't have anything for you—you know, Christmas presents." Her eyes reflected her concern. "Do you think it's too late to head into the village to shop?"

"Yes, I do. They close early in the evenings." He could see his answer only compounded her distress. "Hey, look at me." When she glanced at him, he said, "I don't need any presents. I promise. I have everything I want right here."

He drew her close and placed a quick kiss on her lips.

Serena pulled back. Her eyes opened wide and then a big grin filled her face.

"Oh, no," he said.

"What?"

"You have a look on your face that worries me. I have a feeling I'm not going to like what you say next."

"You can stop worrying. I just got an idea for a new screenplay."

"That's what you were thinking about when I kissed you?"

She shrugged and looked a little sheepish. "I can't help when inspiration strikes."

"Uh-huh. And what is this idea?"

She shook her head. "I'm not telling you. You'll have to wait and read it."

"Really? That's all I get for being your inspiration?"

"Well, maybe if you kissed me some more, you might get something you do like."

Now she was talking his language. "How about we take this to the bedroom?"

"I think that would be a good idea."

The next morning, Serena woke up early.

Jackson was still sound asleep, but that wasn't surprising as he'd had a late night—a very late night. Serena smiled as she recalled the night she'd spent in his arms.

She knew their time together was quickly running out. But she was wondering about relocating to New York, once filming for her next movie wrapped up, of course. After all, she could stand to take a break from movies, and she hadn't yet signed up for anything after this next film. If writing screenplays didn't pan out for her, she could try Broadway. Actually, that was another item on her bucket list. Why put off until tomorrow what she could do today?

The more she thought about the idea, the more she liked it. She just wondered what Jackson would think of the idea. After all, it wasn't like they had to move in together. She could get her own place. They could go slow and see where things were headed.

Slow? Like they'd taken things so far? It sure hadn't been very slow, but she wouldn't change any of the events that got them to this point— well, that wasn't exactly true. She could have avoided the whole Shawn debacle. And she was certain that Jackson would have preferred to skip the accident. But at least he was safe and they were happy together.

She slipped out of bed and put on her fuzzy robe. She quietly padded out of the room and headed for the desk. Her mind was buzzing with thoughts of New York and ideas for her next screenplay. She wanted to get started on notes for it. She decided it was going to be a holiday rom-com.

She opened her laptop and typed in the password. She paused as she realized this would be her second romance. What was up with that? She always thought she would work on a serious drama that dealt with tough issues, but for some reason, it was matters of the heart that spoke to her. Jackson's image came to mind and she smiled. He'd definitely had an influence over her.

And then she realized what she could give him for Christmas—herself. She could wrap up a piece of paper that said something about her being New York–bound. She liked the idea. She just hoped that he would, too.

But first, she had to get some writing done. When her computer booted up, it automatically loaded to her email. It was one thing to skip town and not take calls, but totally sealing herself off from life was another thing altogether. As long as she kept up on her emails and listened to her voice mails, she let herself buy into the illusion that she was on top of things.

The top email in her inbox was from her agent. There was a high-priority flag. Her agent really needed to take some time off and enjoy the holiday. After all, it was Christmas Eve.

The subject line caught and held Serena's attention:

Call me ASAP! Damage control needed!

Damage control? For what? She hadn't been in town for days. There was no way she could have done anything to require such a message. And then she noticed that there was an attachment.

Her agent wasn't an alarmist, so dread was churning in her empty stomach. Her finger hovered over the open button. She knew that once she looked at it that it would cast a cloud over this wonderful holiday season. Was it so wrong for her to want this bit of heaven to last just forty-eight hours more? Besides, who would be looking at the tabloids over the holiday?

She closed her email and opened a new word processing document. She put the email out of her mind and instead concentrated on the idea that had come to her last night while she'd been kissing Jackson.

One of the hardest things for her to write was the opening line. It carried so much weight. It had to snag the viewer's attention. It had to set the tone for the entire movie.

And so Serena typed out a sentence that would be read as part of the heroine's thoughts...

This was to be a Christmas unlike any other.

It was okay. It gave an idea of what was to come. But it didn't pop. It wouldn't stand out and make the viewers forget about their popcorn and soda. Nor would it draw them to the couch to sit down and find out what happened next.

Her mind wandered back to her Christmas present for Jackson. Her mind started playing over all of the various messages that she could write. It could be a long letter, explaining what their time together had meant to her and how she'd been able to regain her trust in her judgment and in men. But that seemed like too much.

Perhaps she should tell him how much fun she'd had with him and that she didn't want it to end. Something like: This wasn't an ending but rather a beginning.

And then she realized the best route was the simplest one. Nine little words would tell him everything he needed to know.

She opened a blank document and started to type. She played with the font size and the color until she ended up with:

My ♥'s in New York...
so I'm moving there.

She made it so the font filled the page and then she printed it. She searched the desk until she found an envelope. Now all she needed was to dress it up. After all, it was a Christmas present of sorts.

But she had no wrapping paper. She would have to be inventive. Her gaze strayed to the Christmas tree and latched on to the red velvet bows attached to the end of random branches. One of those would be perfect.

And so she decorated the envelope and placed

it beneath the Christmas tree. Now she couldn't wait for Christmas. She hoped this present would make him as happy as it did her.

CHAPTER EIGHTEEN

ALONE AGAIN...ON Christmas Eve.

Instead of getting upset over finding the spot next to him empty, Jackson just smiled. He knew last night when Serena got her stroke of genius that it wouldn't be long until she headed to the keyboard to start her next screenplay.

He was proud of her for following her dreams, even though she didn't know for sure how they would turn out. She may be famous, but she was known for her acting, not her writing. There was no guarantee that any production company would get behind her screenplays. But he was excited to know that his interview might help pave this new road for her.

He grabbed his phone to see if his agent had sent him the interview. His fingers moved over the screen until he pulled up the email with the attached video. A smile pulled at his lips. After they'd talked on the phone, Jackson had followed up with an email. He made sure to tell his agent to add music at the beginning as well as some visual narrative. Nothing was to be overlooked. This was that important to him.

Jackson played the video. It was just as he'd imagined—no it was better. And the most striking part was Serena Winston. She was a star, even when she wasn't on the big screen. Beyond her undeniable beauty, there was an air about her—the kind that princesses and queens possessed.

The bedroom door creaked as it opened. Jackson pressed Pause on the video. Then he turned off his phone. There was no way that he was letting her see it. Not yet. This was special and it was his Christmas gift to her.

Serena poked her head inside. "Morning, sleepyhead."

Gizmo squeezed past her, ran into the room with his tail wagging, jumped on the cushioned bench at the end of the bed and then hopped on the bed.

"Arff! Arff!"

"He's been waiting for you to get up. It seems that Gizmo approves of you, which is saying something because he doesn't take to many people. Usually he hides."

Gizmo rushed up to Jackson and before Jackson could move fast enough, Gizmo licked his cheek. "Yes, Gizmo. I like you, too. And it's okay, sometimes I want to hide from people, too." After wiping the wet kiss from his cheek, Jackson turned his attention back to Serena. Their gazes met and he smiled. "I don't even have to ask what happened to you. I can see by that glint in your eyes that the writing is going well."

"It is. And this screenplay is going to be even better than the first one."

"It better be."

"Why do you say that?"

"Because I was the inspiration, remember?"

Her cheeks grew rosy. "I remember." And then she pulled a white pastry box from behind her back. "I have a surprise for you."

His empty stomach rumbled its anticipation. "And what have you been up to besides writing?"

"I drove into the village."

"Did you sleep at all?"

She nodded. "But I'm an early riser."

"You couldn't have gotten much sleep."

She shrugged. "That's what coffee is for. And that reminds me. I picked up some more dark chocolate while I was in the village. I don't know if it's as good as what you bought at the Christmas market, but it was all I could get at that hour of the morning."

He arched a brow. "I take it you really like the cocoa?"

"Oh, yes. What could be better? Chocolate and fresh pastries."

He climbed out of bed. "You don't have to convince me." He threw on some clothes and headed for the door. He paused to place a kiss on her lips. "Well, what are you doing standing there? We have some cocoa to make."

It didn't take long until he had the milk warmed and the chocolate melted into it. With two steamy cups and a box of pastries, they returned to the great room. Serena had started a fire while he was taking care of things in the kitchen. And she'd thought to turn on the Christmas tree lights. It was a very cozy setting, even if the cabin was quite large.

She turned to him on the couch. "Do you know what the best part of a chilly morning is?"

"There's a best part?"

She smiled and nodded. "Snuggling together under a blanket."

He reached for the throw on the back of the couch and snuggled it around Serena before draping what was left over his legs. Gizmo decided it was a good idea and joined them on the couch.

"You know I could get used to this," she said. Jackson leaned toward her and pressed his lips to hers. He didn't say it, but he could get used to this, too. This relationship was so different from the others in his past.

Serena was more than willing to meet him halfway, like her thoughtful trip to the village for breakfast food or her attempt to cook dinner, even though it was a struggle. It didn't matter to him if she'd burned the food, he'd have still loved it, just because she put herself out there for him.

He deepened the kiss. She tasted sweet like chocolate and it had never tasted so good. His hand cupped her face. He never wanted to let her go.

And yes, he knew that their time together was almost at an end. He had a flight back to New York in less than forty-eight hours. When he'd flown to Austria, he hadn't wanted to come. He'd been fully focused on his career and he'd wanted to be any other place but the Alps, where no news ever happened. Instead he'd found something more important—happiness.

He pulled back so that he could look into Serena's eyes. "Do you know how happy you make me?"

She smiled at him. "How happy is that?"

"So happy that I think I want to give you your Christmas present right now." When she frowned, he realized that they'd agreed to forgo presents. "Listen, I know we said that we weren't going to exchange gifts, but this is special. And I hope you really like it—"

"But we can't open gifts."

"Why not?"

"It's not Christmas morning."

"Oh." He hadn't realized that she was a stickler for tradition. And he really didn't want to wait. "Can you make an exception just this once?"

"I suppose." A big grin lit up her face. She looked excited, like a little kid on Christmas morning after Santa left a sled full of presents under the tree. "I got you a present, too."

He struggled to keep from smiling. "You broke the agreement."

"You broke it first."

"True enough." He smiled at her, causing her stomach to dip. "I think you're really going to like my present."

"Open mine first—"

"Not so fast. Maybe we should flip for it."

"Or maybe you should be a gentleman and let the lady go first."

He sighed. "I guess you have me there." He motioned with his hand. "Okay. Go ahead."

She smiled in triumph. "You're really going to like it. The present is under the tree."

He turned but he didn't see anything. "Are you sure?"

"It was right there." She stood and walked over to the tree. She got down on her hands and knees. She looked all around, even under the tree skirt. "It's not here." And then she turned around. "Gizmo."

The dog's ears lowered and he put his head between his paws.

"Don't look so innocent. It's not going to work this time." Serena got to her feet. "Gizmo, how could you do this?"

The pup let out a whine.

Jackson didn't want to see the whole day ruined. "It's okay. It'll turn up. I can give you my present."

"No." And then, as though Serena understood how bad her response sounded, she said, "I'm sorry. I'm just frustrated. I have to find your gift. I can't believe this happened. That dog is such a thief."

Jackson laughed. "I can't argue with that."

"Please help me look for it."

"What am I looking for?"

"You'll know it when you see it. It has your name on the front."

Jackson got down and looked under the couch and then he checked under the armchair. "You know, you could make this a new tradition—

hunting for your Christmas present. I'm sure Gizmo would be glad to help."

"Oh, no. When we get back to the States someone is going back to doggy school. Huh, Gizmo?"

He whined and put his paw over his head.

Jackson chuckled. "I'd like to help you, buddy, but I think she means business."

And sadly, he wouldn't be around to see Gizmo's transformation from an ornery puppy to a well-behaved dog. But more than that, Jackson was going to miss Serena. She was a ray of sunshine in his otherwise bland and gray life.

But before all of that, he had his present for her. While Serena was off searching the kitchen, Jackson pulled out his cell phone to forward her the video. Luckily they'd been talking over lunch yesterday about how to keep in touch and she'd given him her email— *GizmoPuppy007@mymail.com*. He smiled at the address. He didn't think he'd ever forget it—or her.

"I have it."

Serena ran into the great room, waving the envelope around.

"Where did you find it?" Jackson asked as he stood next to the Christmas tree.

"Under the bed. I also found my wallet. I

didn't even know that it was missing…again. I must have put it down when I got back from the bakery and he found it. I also found my hairbrush and one of your socks. He had quite a collection."

"Well, bring it over here." When she approached him and held out the sock, he smiled. "Not that."

She dropped the sock on the floor. "Did you mean this?"

"Yes." He snatched the envelope from her fingers.

She automatically grabbed for it, but he held it out of her reach. "Hey, that wasn't fair."

"Ah…but see, it has my name on it." He pointed to where she'd scrolled his name with a red pen.

"But…" The protest died in her throat. What was she going to say? That she was having an attack of nerves? How would that sound? "Oh, go ahead."

She didn't have to tell him twice. He jabbed his finger into the corner of the envelope and started to rip the seam open. Talk about an overgrown child.

He pulled out the folded piece of paper. His face was void of expression as he read it. His gaze moved to her and then back to the paper. For the longest time, he didn't say anything.

"I don't understand." His eyes studied hers.

Was he serious? She didn't think it was that hard to understand. But if he really needed her to break it down for him, she could do it in three words. "I love you."

Jackson took a step back as though her admission had dealt him a physical blow. "No, you don't."

AKA, he didn't love her back. And by the horrified look on his face, he didn't want her moving to New York, either. Her heart plummeted down to her toes. She blinked repeatedly. She would not cry in front of him. She moved to retrieve the note from his hand, but he took another step away from her.

With his back against the tree, he said, "You can't love me. It's too soon."

Each denial that passed by his lips was like a dagger stabbing into her fragile heart. Her vision blurred. She blinked away the unshed tears and then summoned a steady voice. "I think what you mean to say is that you don't love me."

"I... I..."

"Save it. The truth is written all over your face."

"I tried to tell you that I wasn't ready for a relationship."

"Was that before or after we made love? Or perhaps when you offered to do this interview?

Because I never heard those words. You made it seem like—well, it doesn't matter because I obviously read everything wrong."

"I never meant to hurt you. You've been great. I really appreciate everything you've done—"

She glared at him. "Stop with the kind words." The last thing she could stand now was him being all nice to her. He was yet another man who took what he needed from her heedless of her feelings. "The truth is you think that the time we've spent together was a mistake. One you wish you could forget."

"Serena, I…" He hesitated as he stared at her, seeing that she meant business. "Okay. You're right. I did things and said things that I shouldn't have done. Our time together was great. You're great. But it can't last. You've got to understand. I still love my wife."

The words were pointed and drove straight into her heart. For a moment, she couldn't breathe. So this was it. There was nowhere to go from there. She struggled to keep it all together. She forced herself to take one breath and then another. The last thing in the world she wanted was for him to see just how deeply his words had hurt her.

Serena reached for the note she'd written him and finally snatched it out of his hand. "Now that we've cleared the air. You should go."

She didn't need him to stay and make this worse. There was no way she could compete with a ghost. The ghost would win every time because he could switch up his memories to make his late wife perfect.

And Serena was anything but perfect. Hence, the misguided note in her hand. She clenched her fingers, crunching up the paper.

"Please don't take this personally." Jackson's voice was low. He took a step toward her. "Your note, it was the sweetest, most generous gesture that anyone has ever done for me. Someday you'll find the right man to share that note with. I'm sorry it wasn't me."

Her heart clenched in her chest as she shook her head. "Don't say any more. You're making it worse. Just go."

"You want me to leave now?"

"Yes." She wasn't sure how much longer she could keep her emotions in check. She'd made such a mess of everything.

"Serena, we don't have to end things like this."

"I don't want to work this out. It's not like we're in love. We need to go our separate ways. Now." And then, because she didn't trust herself to keep her rising emotions in check, she said, "I'll be in the kitchen until you're gone."

Gizmo, as though sensing her distress, had

moved to sit at her feet. She bent over and scooped him into her arms. With her head held high, she walked away. After all, she was a Winston—Winstons knew how to maintain their composure—even when their dignity and their hearts had been shredded.

Once in the kitchen with the door shut, she set Gizmo down on the floor. There were no happy barks and no tail wagging. He moved over to the table where Jackson's chair was still pulled out. He settled on the chair and stared at her with those sad puppy eyes.

"Stop looking at me like that," she whispered, feeling guilty for the mess she'd made of all their lives. "Jackson was never going to stay anyway."

Gizmo whined and covered his head with his paw.

Great. Now even the dog was upset with her. You'd think Gizmo belonged to Jackson instead of her. It looked like she wasn't the only one to let down her defenses and fall for the sexy New Yorker.

Serena moved to the window and stared out at the sunny day. The cheeriness of the weather mocked her black mood. She clung to her dark and stormy emotions. It was so much easier to be angry with Jackson than to deal with her broken heart.

She didn't know how much time had passed when she finally plunked down in a chair opposite Gizmo. By then, the pup had dozed off. She was thankful. She didn't think she could take any more of his sad face.

Her phone buzzed. Certain that it was just a friend wishing her a merry Christmas, she leaned over and retrieved it from the kitchen counter. The screen showed that she had four new emails.

Two from friends, one from her agent and one from Jackson—that was strange. What would he send her?

She checked the time stamp, finding the email from Jackson had been sent some time ago—before she'd made an utter fool of herself. What could it be?

And then she recalled him mentioning something about a Christmas gift. Could this have something to do with it?

She hesitated before opening her email. Maybe it would be best to get it over with now. But when she went to click on the email from him, the screen jumped as more graphics loaded. Instead of Jackson's email, the email from her agent opened. Before she could close it, her gaze skimmed over Jackson's name. How would her agent know anything about Jackson being here with her?

The more she read, the worse she felt. Her stomach churned when she got to the end of the email. Jackson had broken his word and had used her interview to further his career. Here she was throwing herself at a man who felt nothing for her and, worse, had lied to her. Once again, her poor judgment had led her into trouble.

She rushed out of the kitchen to confront Jackson, but he was nowhere to be found. When she moved to the window, she saw his rental car pulling out of the driveway.

She told herself it was for the best. There was no way he could undo the fiasco with the video. Right now, it was out there for all the world to see. But even worse than that was the fact that she was in love with a man who didn't love her back.

So much for a merry Christmas…

CHAPTER NINETEEN

THE OUTLINE OF the cabin filled his rearview mirror.

Jackson turned onto the mountain road and headed for the nearby village, hoping that there would be a vacancy. It was Christmas Eve. The village might be full of people visiting for the holidays. If so, he'd keep driving. There was nothing keeping him here.

He told himself he would be fine, even though he felt anything but fine. After all, he hadn't come to Austria to start a relationship. How dare she accuse him of leading her on? He hadn't. He wouldn't. He had made his situation clear to her. Hadn't he? Suddenly he wasn't so sure those words had made it from his thoughts to his lips. When he held Serena in his arms, it was so easy to forget about everything but kissing her.

Just then his phone rang. It was his agent. He didn't really want to talk to him, but it would be best to tell him that the deal with the interview was off. He put the man on speakerphone.

"Hey, Fred, I was about to call you."

"She loved the video, didn't she?" Before Jackson could respond, Fred said, "I knew she would. That's why I took the liberty of releasing it before people got too distracted with Christmas."

"You did what?" Surely Jackson hadn't heard him correctly. He wouldn't go public with the video after Jackson told him how important Serena's privacy was to her.

"Don't worry. It's trending. It's going to hit a million views anytime now—"

"Fred, I told you not to do this!" He was shouting now and he didn't care.

"Relax. I've got your back."

"You're kidding, right? I told you how important this video was to me."

"Of course it's important. That's why I had the best people in the business polish it up before I released it. And let me tell you, after it aired on your network, the video went viral. People are talking about it on every media platform. You're a hero. You found Serena Winston."

"And what about her? Do you know what you've done to her?"

His agent's voice took on an angry tone. "I

didn't do anything to her. She should thank me for her name being on everyone's tongue."

"And did you ever stop to think that if she worked that hard to disappear she might value her privacy?" Serena was going to be so hurt and he'd already done so much damage. He had to do something to fix this.

"Give me some credit. I didn't tell anyone where she is." Fred's voice drew him from his thoughts. "What is up with you? I thought you wanted to do whatever it took to land that evening anchor position? Where is the thank-you?"

"There isn't going to be one. I told you the interview was to be kept under wraps—"

"Wait. You're upset about her, aren't you?"

"No."

"You are. You don't care about the tape being leaked—you care that Serena Winston is upset. What has gotten into you? Where are your priorities?"

"You want to know my priorities? My priority is keeping my word—without it I'm nothing. And I gave Serena my word that I would keep that interview confidential until she decided if or when to go public with her screenplay. And now, thanks to you, everyone and their grandmother knows about Serena's project—a project that she wasn't ready to take public."

"But this will help both of you—believe me,

this is all going to work out. And I didn't tell you the best part. The network executives tuned in. They loved the interview and they want you." When Jackson didn't respond, Fred asked, "Did you hear me?"

"I did. And I don't care. This isn't about me. It's about Serena."

"And she's going to thank you—"

"No. She isn't." Jackson's hands clenched the steering wheel until his knuckles turned white.

"Wow! I've never heard you go off the handle like this."

"If you thought I'd be happy using someone I care about to further my career, you don't know me at all."

"I thought I did. You used to always be so calm and take everything in stride. What has happened to you? It's Serena. She's gotten to you."

"No, she hasn't." Besides, he'd messed things up with her. If he'd had any hope of ever making things right with Serena—this was the final straw.

"Oh, I get it. You're in love with her, aren't you? That's why you're so upset."

He may not be able to do anything about Serena's anger toward him, but he could make sure his agent never leaked a video again.

"Fred, you're fired."

Jackson disconnected the call. He pulled off the quiet mountain road. He got out of his vehicle and just started pacing. He had so much pent-up energy and he just needed to wear it off.

Because there was no way Fred was right. He was not in love with Serena. Sure, he thought she was great. And she had opened his eyes to a life without June, but did that constitute love?

Erase. Erase. Erase.

Serena sat at her desk trying to work on her rom-com screenplay but nothing she wrote was the least bit entertaining. Her heroines were snappy and her heroes were being mulish. It was a disaster.

Her muse was on strike.

And worse yet, her heart was broken. Splintered into a million painful shards.

What had she been doing letting herself get so close to a man who was obviously still in love with his late wife? She should have gotten the hint by the amount of times he'd mentioned June—the love of his life.

And then there was the leaked video. Now that she'd calmed down, she realized it wasn't the disaster she'd originally imagined. Her agent had sent a follow-up email letting her know that there had been numerous read requests for her script.

Jackson may not love her—it had been written all over his face when he'd read the note she'd given him for Christmas. And then he'd tried to gently wiggle out of the idea of them continuing their relationship when they returned to the States.

Even so. He never struck her as a liar or a man who went back on his word. She'd been in the industry long enough to know there were a hundred and one different opportunities to leak a video to the public—

Serena drew her thoughts up short. What was wrong with her? Why was she making excuses for him?

Because whether she wanted to admit it or not, she couldn't hate a man for loving his late wife. It wasn't his fault that someone had laid claim to his heart before Serena had met him.

And perhaps she'd read more into things than she should have. There appeared to be plenty of blame to go around. She thought of talking to him—of setting things straight—but she didn't have his phone number. And at this point, she was probably the last person that he'd want to speak to.

Maybe a year or two from now, when this evening was a distant memory, she'd bump into him during one of her business trips to New York. It would be awkward at first, but perhaps they could get coffee. Maybe they could find their way back to being friends.

A tear splashed onto her cheek. Gizmo rushed over and settled on her lap. Her hand automatically stroked his back, but all she could think about was Jackson and how friendship with him would never be enough.

CHAPTER TWENTY

HE LOVED HER.

He loved her laugh, her smile, and her so-so cooking.

He loved everything about her.

Jackson had thought about nothing else since Serena had tossed him out of her life. And though he hated to admit it, his agent was right. His reaction where she was concerned was way over the top. If that interview had been with anyone else, he would have dealt with it in a more businesslike, more restrained manner. But this interviewee was so much more than a pretty face—she was a breath of fresh air in his otherwise stale life.

And because he'd been too busy trying to impress her, he hadn't slowed down long enough to think about how letting her interview out of his possession could end up being a mess. Jackson paced back and forth in his rented room in the village. He raked his fingers through his hair.

He'd made a gigantic mess of everything. But he refused to give up hope on rectifying his relationship with Serena. After all, wasn't Christmas the season of hope and forgiveness?

He loved Serena Mae Winston.

Not the Hollywood star.

Not the up-and-coming screenplay writer.

But he loved the woman who struggled to cook pasta, who was brave enough to climb in a wrecked car to save a total stranger and who didn't take any gruff from a less than stellar patient.

He grabbed his phone but then realized that he didn't have her phone number. He swore under his breath. What had he been thinking? He should have gotten it a long time ago. Wasn't that one of the first things guys asked for when they were trying to pick up women? It just went to show how long he'd been out of the dating world.

Left with few options, he started typing her a brief email. He had no idea if she would even open it, but he had to try. His thumbs started moving rapidly over the screen of his phone.

Mae. Yes, that's the name of the woman who first caught my attention. It's the name of the person I've come to admire and care a lot about—more than I realized until now.

I guess it's true what they say about not realizing what you've got until it's gone. I made a HUGE mistake and for that I apologize. I wish I could undo so many things, but I can't.

I promise you that I will not take advantage of any opportunities that come my way because of the leaked video. All I want is a chance to show you how sorry I am for not realizing what a precious Christmas present you had given me.

I love—

Erase. Erase.

He didn't want to say too much without seeing her—without being able to gaze into her eyes. He wanted her to see how much she meant to him.

He concluded the email with a simple: Jackson.

His finger hovered over the send button. He reread each word, evaluating its meaning and wondering if he could do anything to make the email more powerful. He knew he was overthinking everything. But this message was all he had at this point.

He knew that she would see the subject line before she pressed Delete. And he only had two words for it.

I'm sorry.

His gut was telling him that this wasn't the right way to do things. He could do better. The cursor moved back and forth between Send and Delete.

He pressed Delete.

He needed to woo her over and an email wouldn't do it. This was going to take him pulling out all of the stops. He had to show Serena how much she meant to him.

It was still early—before noon. Perhaps there would still be some shops open. With a plan in mind, he rushed out of his rented room, down the steps and out the door. The sidewalks were busy with people bustling around with last-minute shopping before the big day.

A group of young people stopped on the sidewalk to sing to a growing audience. Jackson got caught up in the lurkers. He paused to listen to their harmonious and joyful voices. It wouldn't have been so long ago when he would have walked right past such an exhibition, unmoved and uncaring. But he was beginning to see all the wonderful things around him when he slowed down and paid attention.

After their first song, Jackson continued down the sidewalk. Thanks to his visit here with Serena, he remembered a few of the stores in the town square. He just hoped they were still open.

His first stop was the florist. He picked out

every long-stem red rose and for double the usual delivery fee he was able to have them sent to Serena right away. He attached a note:

> *This is only the beginning...*
> J

The singers were still entertaining people as Jackson made his way to the jewelry store. He was going to get Serena a real Christmas present. One that was all wrapped in shiny paper and tied up with a red bow. It would be a gift that told her exactly how he felt about her.

The jewelry store had exactly what he had in mind. And his plan was taking shape. On his way out of the store, he knew what else he needed in order to get Serena's full attention.

CHAPTER TWENTY-ONE

READING WAS GOOD.

They said that it could be an escape from reality. And right now, Serena needed to escape from the mess she'd made of her life. After all, no way did an actress and a television journalist belong together. Just the thought of it would have made her father roll in his grave.

Serena focused on the words on the page. Her eyes scanned the sentence and then the next. By the time she got to the third sentence, she'd forgotten what she'd read in the beginning.

And so she returned to the beginning of the paragraph, intent on reading this reference book on writing screenplays. She really did enjoy writing her first screenplay and though her second had hit a snag, she was certain if she kept at it, the story would come together.

Just over the top of the book, she spotted the large bouquet of red roses that Jackson had sent her. She rested the book against her chest as she continued to stare at the beautiful blossoms nestled in a sea of baby's breath. She'd placed them on the coffee table.

She should probably just get rid of them—out of sight, out of mind. But they were so beautiful. It would be a crime to do away with them.

But it was the attached card that had stirred her interest. What had Jackson meant by saying this was just the beginning? Had he had a change of heart? Were these flowers something that he'd planned before their big blowup? If so, he obviously didn't know that red roses symbolized unconditional love.

Her contemplation came to a halt as she heard not one, but multiple car engines. This was followed by a string of car doors closing. Gizmo awoke from his nap and started his guard dog routine of *bark-bark-howl. Bark-bark-howl.* Repeat. He took off toward the door to defend his home.

Serena tried to hear beyond the dog. It sounded like there was a whole army descending on the cabin—wait, no, not an army.

There was singing.

Christmas carolers?

Serena tossed aside her book and joined the excited Gizmo at the door. She glanced out the window to find the sun had set. Her driveway quickly filled with carolers. They were each holding a candle as they sang. And they were singing in English. Serena was impressed.

She rushed to pull on her coat and boots. Then she attached Gizmo's leash.

She picked up the barking, tail-wagging dog. "Shh...or I'm not taking you outside."

It took a moment, but he quieted down...just until she got outside with him. When he started again, she shushed him. And ran her hand over his back, hoping to calm him.

The singers were amazing. Their voices were beautiful. But what were they doing out here? It wasn't like there were houses lining the road. Dwellings were quite scattered in this particular area. Still, she felt blessed that they would come visit her.

They helped to buoy her flagging spirits. If only Jackson were here with her. She'd bet he'd really enjoy this. But she didn't know where he was. For all she knew, he could be on a flight back to New York.

And then the group parted. It was hard to make out who was walking between them in the dark. Whoever it was, they were approaching the porch. As the person got closer, Serena recognized Jackson. Her heart jumped into her throat. What was he doing here?

She noticed that he was carrying more flowers. The backs of her eyes stung. His image started to blur. She blinked repeatedly. She couldn't believe he was here.

Gizmo wiggled and barked, anxious to get to Jackson. She wasn't the only one happy to see him. She put the dog down. Gizmo immediately ran over to Jackson, who bent down to pet the dog.

In the background, the choir continued to sing. And then Serena realized this was what Jackson had meant by the note with the flowers. He was responsible for bringing the carolers to her door.

He approached her. Their gazes met and held. Her heart started to pound.

"I'm sorry," they both said simultaneously.

Then they both gave an awkward laugh. He held the flowers out to her and she accepted them.

Serena knew she had to say more. She had to make this right. "I overreacted earlier. I was feeling insecure when you didn't like the idea of me moving to New York and I handled it badly."

"You didn't do anything wrong. I did. I totally messed up everything when you gave me that most amazing Christmas present. I panicked. And then I complicated matters by giving your video to my agent to have him get a team to clean it up and give it a polish. I wanted to surprise you with it for Christmas. But my agent got it into his head to leak the video, even though I told him not to. Anyway, he's no longer my agent."

"He's not? Because of me?" She didn't like the thought that she was responsible for someone losing their job.

"No. I let him go because I can't work with someone I don't trust."

"Do you trust me?"

"I do. It's just that I wasn't being honest with myself."

"How so?" She held her breath wondering what he would say.

"I promised June that I would move on—that I'd make a new life for myself. Before she got sick, we'd talked about having kids—a boy and girl. She wanted me to have that chance. She… she thought I'd make a good father. And so she made me promise to marry again. At the time, I would have said anything to make her happy. I didn't think that I could take a chance on love again—the loss—the pain. I didn't want to love anyone ever again. And then I met you. Do you know what you've taught me?"

Serena shook her head.

"I learned that it's a very lonely life without

someone to share it with. And I don't want to hide from the truth."

"What truth would that be?"

He stepped closer to her. He reached out and stroked his fingers over her cheek. "The undeniable truth is that I love you, Serena Mae Winston."

"You do?"

"I do."

She at last drew in a full breath. "I love you, too."

He pulled her close and kissed her. It was the sweetest, most meaning-filled kiss of her life. She didn't know why it took traveling halfway around the globe to find her soul mate, but she'd do it again. At last, she felt as though she was right where she belonged.

When Jackson pulled back, he looked her right in the eyes. "Do you trust me?"

She knew what he was asking. If his career would come between them. "Do you plan to share with the world details of our private lives?"

"Only the pieces that we agree on sharing."

"Then yes, I trust you." She knew in that moment that her father had rolled over in his grave with a very loud groan, but she wouldn't let that stop her. Her father had died alone. She didn't want to end up like him. She wanted to learn from her father's mistakes.

In the background, the carolers had moved on to a slower song in German. Even though she understood only a few words, it was still a beautiful harmony.

Jackson pulled a little box from his pocket. It was wrapped in shiny silver paper with a red bow. It looked like a jewelry box. What exactly had he done?

He held it out to her. "This is for you. It is a proper Christmas present to replace the one that was ruined. I hope you like it."

Her fingers trembled slightly as she undid the ribbon and the paper. It was indeed a little black box from a jeweler's. The breath caught in her throat. When she lifted the lid, she found a black velvet box—a box bigger than one that holds a ring.

Jackson held the wrappings so that she could use her hands to open the last box. Inside was a silver heart locket. It was engraved with a beautiful design. It was delicate and attached to a thin box chain.

"It's beautiful." Tears of happiness filled her eyes. She glanced up at him. "Thank you."

"You have my heart for now and always."

"And you have mine."

"Arff! Arff!"

Jackson stuffed the wrapping paper and

empty boxes in his pockets. Then he bent over and scooped Gizmo up in his arms.

Serena leaned forward and hugged her two favorite guys. "We love you, too, Gizmo."

"Arff!"

EPILOGUE

One year later...

"I can't believe you were able to lease the same cabin."

Jackson carried Serena over the threshold. "I wanted everything to be special for my Christmas bride."

She turned to look into her husband's eyes. "You didn't have to bring me to Austria for it to be special. You do that all by yourself."

Serena leaned forward and pressed her lips to his. She'd never tire of kissing him. Ever.

Jackson was everything she'd never thought she'd have. He was her best friend. He lent her an ear when she needed to vent. He offered a word of reason when she was worked up. And he was the person who filled her life with much laughter and tons of love. And she could only hope she did the same for him.

Their lives had been evolving over the past

year. She'd filmed her last contracted movie and was now concentrating on her writing, which meant she could relocate to New York. Jackson had been promoted to the anchor chair of the evening news for the biggest network in the country. He had more control over the content than ever before and he was very happy. They both were deliriously happy.

"Arff! Arff!"

Reluctantly, she pulled back. Jackson gently set her feet on the floor.

Serena knelt down and ran a hand over Gizmo. "You are special, too."

"Arff!"

Serena couldn't help but laugh. "I still think Gizmo understands exactly what we say."

"I think you're right."

She straightened and walked into the great room. "I can't believe that yesterday we were with your mother next to the Pacific Ocean where we exchanged vows. And today we are in the Alps. I'm so glad you patched things up with her."

"I'm glad I'm smart enough to listen to my very intelligent wife with her wise advice."

"Aw…" She approached him and wrapped her arms around his trim waist. "You know exactly what to say." She pressed a quick kiss to his lips.

"Look." Jackson gestured toward the window. "The snow I ordered is just starting—"

"It is?" She rushed over to the window. "It is." She turned back to Jackson. "Something tells me if you have any pull with Mother Nature this will turn into a snowstorm."

"You bet. It worked well the first time around."

"You consider a car accident working well?"

He shrugged. "It brought you into my life, didn't it?"

A smile tugged at Serena's lips. "It did, but I'd prefer if you didn't get hurt this time around."

"I'll see what I can do about that. Maybe if we hide away in this cabin, you can keep an eye on me." His eyes had a playful twinkle in them.

"I think you have a good idea." She stepped farther into the room. "Oh, look, a Christmas tree." She turned back to Jackson. "Did you do this?"

He nodded. "I know how much you enjoy the holiday."

"But it isn't decorated."

"I thought you'd enjoy doing it." Then he pulled something from his pocket. "And I have the first ornament."

He handed it to her. She glanced down at the cake topper from their wedding. It was a winter bride and her dashing groom; the bride was dressed in white with a hood and cape, and holding red roses. The cake topper now had a small brass hook with a red ribbon strung through it.

Serena's gaze rose to meet her husband's. "Did you think of everything?"

"I tried."

She slipped off her coat and rushed over to the tree where the ladder was waiting. She climbed up to find the perfect spot for the ornament. It took her a moment to decide. "There. Isn't it perfect?"

"Yes." And then he started to gently shake the ladder.

"Jackson. Stop." She held on so she didn't fall. "What are you doing?"

"The last time you were up on that ladder, you fell into my arms. I just want a repeat."

She frowned at him. "Stop playing around."

"I won't drop you. I promise."

"That's good, because I have a Christmas present for you. I hope you like it."

He arched a brow. "I thought we agreed not to get each other anything since we were going to be on our honeymoon."

"I didn't go shopping for it. I promise."

"So you made me a gift?" There was a look of intrigue reflected in his eyes.

"In a manner of speaking." Happiness and excitement bubbled up in her chest. "Merry Christmas, Daddy."

His eyes opened wide. "Daddy?"

The breath caught in her throat. This hadn't been planned, but she knew he wanted children. She just didn't know if he wanted them now.

Please be excited. Please. Oh, please.

Why wasn't he saying anything? Was he in shock?

"Jackson?" She snapped her fingers. "Jackson, speak."

"I... I'm going to be a dad?"

A hesitant smile lifted her lips as she nodded. "Does that make you happy?"

At last, his lips lifted at the corners. "Oh, yes. That makes me very happy. Come here, Mrs. Bennett."

She started to climb down the last couple of rungs on the ladder, but her feet never touched the floor as her husband swept her into his arms. His lips pressed to hers. He left no doubt in her mind just how happy he was about this news.

And then he pulled back ever so slightly. "What do you say we trim the tree later?"

"Why, Mr. Bennett, what do you have on your very naughty mind?" She laughed.

"As I recall, you like my naughty mind."

"Mmm-hmm…" She smiled up at him.

And with that he carried her to the master suite to begin their happily-ever-after.

* * * * *

If you enjoyed this story, check out these other great reads from Jennifer Faye:

MARRIED FOR HIS SECRET HEIR
THE MILLIONAIRE'S ROYAL RESCUE
HER FESTIVE BABY BOMBSHELL
THE GREEK'S NINE-MONTH SURPRISE

All available now!

Get 2 Free Books,

HARLEQUIN *superromance*

Plus 2 Free Gifts—
just for trying the Reader Service!

Get 2 Free Books,

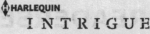

Plus 2 Free Gifts—

just for trying the Reader Service!

HI17R